CONN DURY

He'd come through all sorts of trouble.

His father and mother had been massacred by Apaches when he was nine. He'd been an Apache slave for three years until he broke free.

He'd seen no-goods, drifters, gunslingers and killers-for-money.

But the railhead town was the first place he'd run up against a skunk who'd shoot a woman.

Bantam Books by Louis L'Amour

Ask your bookseller for the books you have missed

BENDIGO SHAFTER
BORDEN CHANTRY
BRIONNE
THE BROKEN GUN
THE BURNING HILLS
THE CALIFORNIOS
CALLAGHEN
CATLOW
CHANCY
CONAGHER
DARK CANYON
DOWN THE LONG HILLS
THE EMPTY LAND
FAIR BLOWS THE WIND
FALLON
THE FERGUSON RIFLE
THE FIRST FAST DRAW
FLINT
GUNS OF THE TIMBER-
  LANDS
HANGING WOMAN
  CREEK
THE HIGH GRADERS
HIGH LONESOME
HOW THE WEST WAS
  WON
THE IRON MARSHAL
THE KEY-LOCK MAN
KID RODELO
KILLOE
KILRONE
KIOWA TRAIL
THE MAN CALLED
  NOON
THE MAN FROM
  SKIBBEREEN
MATAGORDA
THE MOUNTAIN
  VALLEY WAR
NORTH TO THE RAILS
OVER ON THE DRY SIDE

THE PROVING TRAIL
THE QUICK AND THE
  DEAD
RADIGAN
REILLY'S LUCK
THE RIDER OF LOST
  CREEK
RIVERS WEST
SHALAKO
SILVER CANYON
SITKA
TAGGART
TUCKER
UNDER THE SWEET-
  WATER RIM
WAR PARTY
WESTWARD THE TIDE
WHERE THE LONG GRASS
  BLOWS

Sackett Titles by
Louis L'Amour

1. SACKETT'S LAND
2. TO THE FAR BLUE
  MOUNTAINS
3. THE DAYBREAKERS
4. SACKETT
5. LANDO
6. MOJAVE CROSSING
7. THE SACKETT
  BRAND
8. THE LONELY MEN
9. TREASURE
  MOUNTAIN
10. MUSTANG MAN
11. GALLOWAY
12. THE SKY-LINERS
13. THE MAN FROM THE
  BROKEN HILLS
14. RIDE THE DARK
  TRAIL

KIOWA TRAIL
LOUIS L'AMOUR

BANTAM BOOKS
TORONTO · NEW YORK · LONDON

KIOWA TRAIL

A Bantam Book | October 1964

2nd printing .. December 1968	4th printing ...... January 1970
3rd printing .... June 1969	5th printing .... April 1970
6th printing .... July 1970	

New Bantam edition | August 1971

2nd printing .. November 1971	9th printing .... January 1976
3rd printing .... May 1972	10th printing ...... August 1977
4th printing .. November 1972	11th printing .... May 1978
5th printing .... August 1973	12th printing .... April 1979
6th printing .... August 1974	13th printing .... January 1980
7th printing .... April 1975	14th printing .... May 1980
8th printing .. December 1975	15th printing ..September 1980
16th printing .... August 1981	

*Cover photo of Louis L'Amour by
John Hamilton—Globe Photos, Inc.*

*All rights reserved.
Copyright © 1964 by Bantam Books, Inc.
This book may not be reproduced in whole or in part, by
mimeograph or any other means, without permission.
For information address: Bantam Books, Inc.*

ISBN 0-553-20518-8

Published simultaneously in the United States and Canada

Bantam Books are published by Bantam Books, Inc. Its trademark, consisting of the words "Bantam Books" and the portrayal of a rooster, is Registered in U.S. Patent and Trademark Office and in other countries. Marca Registrada. Bantam Books, Inc., 666 Fifth Avenue, New York, New York 10103.

PRINTED IN THE UNITED STATES OF AMERICA

25 24 23 22 21 20 19 18 17 16

To Lieut. Ambrose Freeman,
my great-grandfather, who lost his scalp
to the Sioux, Dakota Territory, 1863.

"We rode a Kiowa Trail, him and me,
with Winchesters to point the way."
— from the diary of Jordan Rascoe.

CHAPTER 1

We came up the trail from Texas in the spring of '74, and bedded our herd on the short grass beyond the railroad. We cleaned our guns and washed our necks and dusted our hats for town, riding fifteen strong to the hitching rail and standing fifteen strong to the bar.

We were the Tumbling B from the rough country of the Big Bend, up the trail with three thousand head of longhorn steers, the first that spring, although the rivers ran bank-full and Comanches rode the war trail.

We had buried two hands south of the Red and one on the plains of the Nation. A fourth had died on Kansas grass, his flesh churned under a thousand tearing hoofs. Two men had fallen before Comanche rifles, but the Comanches sang their death songs in the light of a hollow moon, and the Kiowas mourned in their lodges for warriors who fell before the guns of the Tumbling B.

The town to which we had come was ten buildings long on the north side of the street, and seven long on the south, with stock corrals to the east, and a Boot Hill on the west, and in between an edging from the mills of hell.

South of the street were the shacks of the girls,

1

and north of it the homes of the respectable business-men of the town, where no trail driver was per-mitted to go.

We were the riders who drove the beef on which the town's existence was built, fighting dust, hail, and lightning, meeting stampede and Kiowa lance, leaving the Comanche dead in his own tall grass. We fought our nameless Alamos and rode to our deaths without a song of glory, nor any memory to leave behind except a hand less at the night guard and an empty saddle in the chuck wagon.

We rode the long grass miles where no boundaries were, some riding a day's work for a day's pay, but others filled with their own wild poetry, conscious of the epic they rode.

Wild and hard were the men of the Tumbling B. Only two of us were past thirty, and some not yet twenty. We meant money to the girls of the Line and whiskey sales to the bartenders; to the merchants we were lean, brown young savages whose brief assault on their town was tolerated because of the money we brought.

That was the year I was thirty-five, and only the cook was as old as I. It was my fifth trip up the trail. I'd seen this town born from the stock pens, and other towns before it. At least one of those towns I'd seen die, leaving only brief scars for the prairie grass to erase.

We rode up the trail as before, with Kate Lundy driving her army ambulance alongside the chuck wagon, and when the Kiowas attacked, Kate's buffalo gun boomed an echo to our own.

That was the year when young Tom Lundy was nineteen, as much of a man as any man could wish to be, and he had left no love back in Texas.

He was one among us who rode north with a dream.

For he wanted a girl, not just one to hold in his arms for a passing hour, but one to whom he could speak in the moonlight, a girl eager for the bright beauty of new love, with ears to listen to the words born of the poetry of life that had awakened within him.

And I, who had ridden beside him and seen him grow from the boy he'd been to the man he had become, knew what lay within him, knew the better because my heart had been singing its own song, and my horse's hoofs had drummed a tune to the sound of the same haunting, far-off bells.

The girl stood on the boardwalk outside the store, and when she lifted a hand to shade her eyes toward us, the sun caught at the red lights in her hair, and her eyes reached out for Tom as he rode up the street.

She looked straight at him, with a smile on her face, and at nineteen the smile of a strange girl is a glory to the blood and a spark to the spirit, carrying a richer wine than any sold across the bar of a frontier saloon.

He'd had no shave for days, and the dust of the trail lay thick on his clothing, but he stepped down from the saddle and walked toward her. She looked at him, a long, appraising look, and then she turned and went inside. The glance she left with him neither promised nor rejected.

He had taken his hat off, and now his hair blew in the wind. He stood there staring, his heart yearning after her. Up the street John Blake was watching, the black cigar in his teeth, and then his eyes turned to me. He rolled his cigar to the other side of his mouth, then turned away and walked up the street.

Tom came back to his horse. "Conn," he said excitedly, "did you see her? Did you see that girl?"

"I saw her."

He wanted a bath and a shave, he wanted new clothes ... and he wanted to know that girl.

"It's trouble you're facing, Tom Lundy," I said. "She was a bonny lass, but you know the rules. No trail hand may walk north of the street, nor disturb the citizens."

"I've got to know her, Conn. I've got to! I'm not going to bother anybody. It's just that I've got to know her, to talk to her."

"This is John Blake's town."

The name had a special sound of its own, for it was a name known wherever cattle grazed. He was a hard man, trained by experience in the handling of hard men, knowing as much of their ways and movements as we knew of the cattle we drove. When he spoke, his voice was law. A square, powerful man with square, powerful hands, a man with a reputation for square dealing, but one who backed his law with a gun.

"This is a time for courting," Tom Lundy said, "and I want trouble with no man—least of all with John Blake."

When we stepped down from our saddles at the Bon Ton, I heard Red Mike say, "No drinking this day. We've got a man to stand behind."

There was a bright eagerness in young Tom's eyes, and I stood there on the walk, watching him, and thinking about it.

Tom Lundy was a man—man-strong, and man in the work he did. He was Kate Lundy's brother, but he had asked no favors because of it, standing to his work through drouth and blizzard, through dust and Indian battle. Yet in some ways he was very young, for in our wild country there were no girls for miles, and none for the likes of young Tom, who had grown to manhood on the novels of Sir Walter Scott.

In his own dreams he was a knight in bright armor who rode to find the golden-haired princess. He was no fool, no wild-eyed idealist, but simply a strong young man with an honest dream, a dream that his sister—and I, God help me—had helped to build.

And he had seen the girl.

It might have been any of a thousand girls in a thousand towns spread across the land, but the moment was here, and it was this one he had seen.

Bannion came out of his saloon and paused beside me. "Hard drive, Conn?"

"The usual . . . more Indians, I think."

"You're the first up the trail."

"Ban," I said, "there was a girl in front of the store over there, a tall, straight, fine-looking girl with a touch of red in her hair. Do you know who she might be?"

"Stay away from her."

"It's not me. It's young Tom."

Bannion took the cigar from his teeth and studied it carefully before replying. "Conn, you tell the boy to stay on his own side of the street. That's Aaron McDonald's daughter."

The sign was on the store into which she had walked: *McDonald's Emporium.*

"Tom Lundy," I said, "is a fine lad. If I had a sister I'd be proud to have Tom interested in her."

Bannion put the cigar back in his mouth and relighted it. "Tom Lundy," he said then, "is a Texan. He's also a cattle driver. In the mind of Aaron McDonald that rates him a mite lower than a red Indian."

"The hell with him."

"All right . . . but you take my advice. Tell Tom to lay off."

"Did you ever try to talk to a youngster who has just seen the girl he thinks he can't live without?"

"Aaron McDonald is a stiff-necked, bigoted old Puritan." Bannion spoke softly, and that very fact conveyed something to me. "He owns the Emporium, he owns a piece of the bank, he owns the livery stable. He also has the finest house in town, with grass growing in the yard and a picket fence around it.

"He came to town eight months ago, and he passes me on the walk two or three times a day. He has never spoken to me, he has never so much as acknowledged my existence."

Bannion paused. "I want you to understand something, Conn. I know how he feels, and do not hold it against him.

"He's eastern. Since he came into town he hasn't once driven any further out of town than the cemetery. When he came west he brought his New England village mind right along with him. He's a hard man, Conn, and, meaning no offense, he thinks cattlemen are a wild, lawless crowd."

In spite of myself, I had to smile. Sure, some of us were wild and lawless . . . this had been, and still was to a great extent, a lawless country.

"Tom's a good boy," I said. "One of the best."

"Not to Aaron McDonald, he isn't. You put chaps and spurs on a man, and as far as McDonald is concerned, he's a savage.

"He says the cattle are a passing phase, and the sooner we're rid of them, the better. And believe it or not, there are plenty who think just as he does."

"Out *here?* They're crazy!"

"They are looking to farmers, Conn. They want

to be rid of the cattle business, and of my kind, too, when it comes to that."

"They're jumping the gun, if you ask me. It will be years before there's farmers enough in this country to support a town."

"Not to hear them tell it."

Kate Lundy was coming out of the hotel, so I excused myself and went to meet her.

Kate was a handsome woman. Not all the hardship of pioneering on the Texas border had taken one bit of it from her. She was tall, slender, and graceful. She had a beautifully boned face and large, lovely eyes . . . yet there was a kind of special steel in Kate Lundy, a steel tempered and honed by the need to survive under the harshest kind of conditions. Only two people knew what Kate had been through . . . only one, really, for Tom had been too young to appreciate most of it. And that left me.

"Good morning, Conn," Kate said. "How are the cattle?"

"Fine. I left Priest and Naylor out there with D'Artaguette."

"Have you had breakfast?"

"Coffee . . . I thought I'd better come in and talk to them first. Hardeman's down at the yards. He can handle five hundred head today, but we'll have to graze most of the herd until he gets more cars."

"The grass is good."

"Yes . . . it is."

"You're worried, Conn. What is it?"

"Tom. He's laid his eyes on Aaron McDonald's daughter, and he's cleaning up to go courting."

"You mean she isn't a nice girl? Is that it?"

"She lives north of the street."

She didn't reply for a minute or two, and we stood

there together in the bright sunlight. Finally, she said simply, "Conn, let's have breakfast."

We turned toward the restaurant, but John Blake was coming up the walk, and we stopped to greet him.

He had a square, strong face and blue eyes, cool eyes that measured a man with care. He wore a neat black suit with a black tie.

"How do you do?" he said to Kate. "Mrs. Lundy, is it?"

"Yes, and you'll be John Blake."

His eyes flickered to me. "And you are Conn Dury."

Oh, he knew the name, all right! There were not many in the cattle country who didn't, and there were both good and bad things he could have heard of me. Being John Blake, he had heard it all, I think. He would make it his business to do so.

"You've the name of a good cattleman, Dury, and your steers look it." He glanced along the street, and then he came to the point. "Your men aren't drinking."

"No."

"Tod Mulloy," he said, "and Red Mike . . ."

"And a dozen more like them. They're good men, John Blake."

"You came for trouble, Dury."

"The Comanches are riding the war trail, and the Kiowas. A man would be a fool not to expect trouble."

"No more?"

"Man," I said irritably, "think of it. Why would we want trouble? Mrs. Lundy has a good crew, a solid crew, and a crew that has been with her for some time. Our hands are her family."

"It is true, Mr. Blake," Kate said.

He was not through. He knew as well as we did

that when hands do not drink something is in the wind, and he wanted to know what to expect.

We were scarcely seated in the restaurant before she came in—a beautiful girl, cool, composed, and a bit older than I had first thought. She was perhaps nineteen, or even twenty, and few girls reached that age without being married. Kate glanced at her, then looked again, but before she could say anything to me the door burst open and Tom came in.

He did not see us. He saw nothing but the girl before him, seated alone at a table. He approached her, sweeping his hat fom his head.

"I saw you when I rode into town," he said. "I am a poor hand for courting, knowing little but horses, cattle, and grass. I only know that when I saw you standing there, I knew that my life began and ended with you, and I would have no happiness until I knew you."

She looked up at him and said, "My father is Aaron McDonald, and a hard man. He looks with no favor on Texas men."

"If you will allow it, I shall call this evening."

"The house stands among the cottonwoods at the street's far end," she said, and then she added, "and it is north of the street."

"You can expect me," he said.

He turned and walked out of the restaurant, and he did not see us, nor look our way.

She sat very still after he had gone, and there was no change of color in her face, although I noticed a brightness in her eyes that I did not like.

The girl who brought us our food was young, a pretty girl with a pert, attractive face. She paused in passing by the other girl's table.

"That was no nice thing to do, Linda," she said, "and well you know it. He is a Texas man, and John

Blake will allow no Texas man north of the street."

"What's the matter, Moira? Jealous?"

The waitress turned away sharply and brought our food to us.

Linda got up and, with a brief smile in our direction, walked out. Immediately, Moira stepped up to our table again. "If he is a friend of yours, that Texas cowboy," she said, "tell him not to go north of the street tonight."

"Thank you," Kate said. "He is my brother."

"Oh—" She flushed. "I'm sorry, I shouldn't have interfered, but it's awful, what she does! Why, if she really cared for anybody—I mean, if a girl really cared, she'd come south of the street to see him."

"Would *you?*" Kate asked.

Her chin lifted. "Yes, ma'am, I would! If a man wanted so much to see me—I mean if he talked to me like that—I'd go south of the street to see him! *Any* street!"

"I wish it were you he was going to see," Kate said.

We went on sitting there, and Kate looked across the table at me. "Conn . . . what can we do?"

"I will see John Blake."

I saw the flicker of worry in her eyes. "Conn, be careful. I want no trouble."

"With Blake? Each of us knows too much about the other. We can talk without guns."

"All right."

"He's a good man, Kate," I said. "Tom, I mean. You've done a fine job."

"*I* have? You mean, *you* have, Conn. Whatever he is, you made him. He worshiped you, and he still does."

"It was you."

She put down her cup. "Conn? Do you remember that day? You saved us all then. It was like a miracle."

The only miracle was what happened to me, for I was running then, running wild and loose with nothing behind me but trouble, and nothing before me but the expectation of more.

Behind me lay the Rio Grande. My horse was scarcely dry from the crossing when I heard the hollow boom of the guns, and knew what it was, for I'd cut the Apache trail south of the border twice in the past few days, and each time had come upon the sort of hell that only an Apache could leave behind.

Lonely ranch houses burned, the stock run off, the dead and mutilated bodies left behind in the sun. Each time they had come upon people at work, people expecting no trouble, but from the sound of that gun I had an idea they had failed in another surprise attack.

There had been nine Indians in the party whose trail I had cut. From the rocks I looked out and saw the flames of a burning house, the rising smoke . . . and nearer to me I saw the Apaches.

Near the house one lay sprawled in death, or what seemed to be death. Nearer to me still, one crawled with a broken leg.

The buffalo gun boomed again, and from the smoke I located the lone fighter . . . it was a woman!

And then behind her, the "dead" Apache moved. And when he moved, I fired.

There was no thought behind the action, no reasoning, no desire to help. The Apache was behind the woman, and he was rising up, knife in hand. My rifle simply came up and I fired.

He screamed, and threw himself blindly forward, but he was already dead even as he fell near the woman.

At least two of the nine Apaches were accounted for, which left seven, but my position was a good one. Before firing, I had already, almost automatically, located the positions of most of them. So with the sound of my own shot in my ears I knew I had declared war, and the only way out was victory. Turning swiftly, I fired three times, as rapidly as the gun could be triggered.

My attack was too sudden for them, too unexpected. My first shot took an Indian between the shoulders; the second splattered sand; the third caught a leaping, running Indian in full stride, and he fell, throwing his rifle out before him.

An Indian is not under any compulsion to fight to the last man. When the odds are against him, he simply slips away, if it is possible to do so, and waits to fight another day. Three men out of nine were dead, and at least one wounded. The spirits were not with them, so they faded away into the brush, taking with them their dead that they could reach.

Mounting up, I rode down to meet Kate Lundy for the first time.

"Maybe if I talked to Tom?" Kate suggested suddenly.

"Kate, the boy's riding a dream. He's seen a girl, and at this moment she looks to him like all the girls he's ever dreamed of. The fact that there's opposition only makes it seem more right. You can talk if you wish, but it will do no good."

After a minute, I added, "And I wouldn't give a tinker's damn for him if it did."

Taking up my hat, I got to my feet. "Hardeman will be ready to talk business," I said. "Do you want me there?"

"I can handle it."

"Then I'll see John Blake."

CHAPTER 2

Tod Mulloy and Red Mike were loitering on the edge of the walk near the Emporium. They got up as I came near. Tod was twenty-two, and had been punching cows on Texas range since he was fourteen. He and Tom Lundy rode as saddle partners. Red Mike was a tough hand, a good man with a rope and with any kind of stock. He was also a very good man with a gun . . . and he didn't scare.

"Conn," Mike asked roughly, "are they going to make trouble for that boy?"

"I'll talk to John Blake."

"He won't take any talk. You know how he is, Conn. With him a rule is a rule."

"I'll handle him."

"Well," Mike said, "if anybody can, you can."

"Not that way," I said irritably. "This mustn't run into gun trouble, so you sit tight."

"If you need us," Mike said, "we'll be here. And sober."

John Blake was in the Bon Ton. When I walked in the door he took his bottle from the bar and reached over for a couple of glasses. Together we walked to a back table and sat down.

"You sold your beef?"

"Kate's talking to Hardeman."

Blake filled two glasses. "Conn, do me a favor? When you get your money . . . pull out."

"Kate's the boss. We move when she says we move."

"She'll listen to you."

"Maybe."

"Conn, you've got a tough crew. I know some of your boys. I knew them in Abilene and in Ellsworth, and I know when to expect trouble. When a crew like yours isn't drinking, there's something wrong. I want to know what it is."

"Were you ever in love, John? I mean when you were a kid?"

He looked startled. Come to think of it, I think it was the only time I ever saw John Blake startled by anything. He was suddenly embarrassed, too.

"Hell, everybody's been in love. Or thought he was."

"Which amounts to the same thing."

John touched his mustache with a finger and studied me, so I put it to him straight, right across the board.

"John, Tom Lundy's going north of the street tonight."

His face stiffened and his eyes became like marbles. "No," he said. "I will not permit it."

"There are other ways to look, John. You don't have to see it happen, and there'll be no trouble."

"You don't know what you're talking about. Hell, if I'd guessed that was what the trouble was, I'd—"

"Tom Lundy's Kate's brother, John. He's one of the very best. He's no wild kid. He's hard-working, he's serious, and he's a boy who's going to do well in the world. Believe me, any girl who wouldn't be interested in him would be off her head."

"Have you ever met Aaron McDonald?"

"No."

"Well . . . meet him. You'll see what I mean. He's

a hard man, a rigid man. There's no give in him anywhere, and there's only black or white so far as he's concerned. He's a witch burner."

"I don't get you."

"A witch burner. Like those people back in the old days. This is a man who could pass sentence and light the fires himself. Yet in his way he's a good, solid citizen. He was against hiring me, but he's pleased because since they hired me there's been no gun trouble in town, and everybody from the Texas crowd has stayed south of the street.

"He helped raised money for the church, and before we had a preacher he spoke from the pulpit. He's a hell and damnation man, and one of his sermons was about Texas men. He's rabid on the subject . . . that, and making money."

"How does he figure to make money if he doesn't cater to the cattlemen?"

"Hell, Conn, where else can the cattlemen go? This is the best shipping point, and McDonald and his crowd know it. And remember this: he isn't alone. Two-thirds of the town stand right with him. Tallcott, Braley, Carpenter—all that crowd. Tallcott came west with McDonald, and so did Braley. They can muster forty men to stand against you, perhaps more."

"There will be no trouble with Tom unless somebody else makes it. He thinks he's found the girl he's been dreaming about, and maybe he has."

"He hasn't."

Something in his tone made me look right at him. "Care to make that clear?"

John Blake's pale, hard face colored a mite. "I'm not one to talk about a woman. Did this boy tell you what she said?"

"We heard it, Kate and me. She didn't say to come, she didn't say not to come."

"So, you see."

"What?"

"She's in the clear." John Blake shifted in his seat and leaned his thick forearms on the table. "Conn, I'd not want these words repeated, but that girl's going to get somebody killed. In fact, that may be what she has in mind."

"You're crazy!" I said. It was a foolish idea. I'd seen the girl, and she was as much of a lady as a man would care to see. Nothing flighty about her, and no question about it, she was lovely. Maybe a little cool . . . but that kind sometimes are the most passionate, sometimes the most affectionate.

"I've seen the girl, John," I added.

"Don't take me wrong. There's never been a word against her. She doesn't go riding out with young men and get herself talked about. Why, I can count the times on my fingers when she's even walked down the street with a young man."

We were getting nowhere, and Kate might need me to talk to Hardeman—although she never had. Kate was a shrewd business woman, and no nonsense about her. In her own way, Kate could be as tough or as hard as any man. She'd had to be.

"And that's just the trouble."

"What?"

"Look, Conn. Here's a mighty pretty girl. She's twenty years old, although I don't think she admits to it. This here is a country where most girls marry at sixteen to eighteen, and believe me, she's had chances.

"Like I've said, she doesn't go riding with them, she doesn't walk out with them. She invites them home. Or lets them believe they were invited."

"So?"

"Then her father sends them away."

It made no kind of sense to me, and I said as much. John Blake pushed his hat back on his head, then took it off and put it on the table beside him.

"Maybe I'm not making myself clear. The point is, I don't think she *wants* to get married, and I think she *likes* to have her father send these men away. And he does. Oh, believe me, he does!"

Blake paused, and then he said, "Conn, I don't know whether this makes sense to you or not, but I think she hates men."

Right then I began to wish Kate Lundy was here. When it comes to cattle, horses, or men, I can handle them. I know all about them, but I've never had much truck with women. Give me a good old fist fight, knuckle-and-skull in the street, and I'll handle my share. Or I'll take a herd over a bad trail and bring them through in as good shape as any man.

"That doesn't make sense."

Blake tossed off his drink. "Conn, if you'd spent your life dealing with trail-town people the way I've done, you'd find a lot of things don't make sense.

"You talk to that boy. You tell him about her, and keep him south of the street."

"And if I can't?"

"Then I'll have to stop him myself."

There it was . . . laid right on the line.

"This isn't a challenge, John. You can look the other way for once. Just don't see him. Let the boy get over there and find out for himself, and let him get back. Then we'll ride out of town and there'll be an end to it."

He looked at me. "You think it is that easy? Break that rule once—just *once*—and there's no more rule. I'd be in a shooting every night in the week all during the season. If one man can go over, why can't they all?"

We sat there knowing our talk was over and we'd gotten nowhere, yet we were reluctant to get up and walk away, because we both knew that when we did the bars were down and trouble was smoking.

"John, I'm asking you. Look the other way."

"I can't. And if I could, McDonald wouldn't. Believe me, Conn, there's no give to the man. He's like iron."

My mouth was dry and my hands felt awkward and empty on the table before me. The whiskey was there, but I'd no wish for it. Liquor never solved any problem, nor did it make a problem more simple.

"John, if the kid goes north of the street—"

He looked at me. Those cold eyes colder still. "If he goes north of the street . . . what?"

"I'll back him, John."

For a long minute we looked across the table at each other, and each knew what the moment meant. John Blake was a trail-town marshal whose reputation depended on fearlessness. He was a good man with a gun, but a man who used one sparingly. He never threatened, never swaggered, never laid a hand on a gun unless to draw it, and never drew unless to shoot. And he never shot unless to kill.

And in the course of fifteen years as a shotgun guard on Wells-Fargo stages and marshal of cow towns, John Blake had killed eleven men. None of them had been drunks or reputation-seeking youngsters. There were other ways of handling *them*.

As for myself, John Blake knew enough about me to understand what the decision might mean. There had been a time—although I had never asked for such a reputation—when it was said that I was a faster man than Wes Hardin, and the most dangerous man alive.

"I shall regret that," he said simply, and I knew the man well enough to know he meant it.

"Tom Lundy is the son I'd like to have had," I said, "although I'm scarcely old enough to be his father."

He nodded, acknowledging that it was high praise. After a minute he said, "Can you keep your boys out of it, Conn? I've heard talk of men treeing a western town, but you know and I know that it never happened. It never could happen in a town where seventy per cent of the town's citizens are war veterans, and ninety per cent have fought Indians.

"Aaron McDonald now—don't underrate the man. He's a cold fish, but he's got nerve, and if he thought I'd need it he would back me with fifty rifles, every man-jack of them a dead shot."

He looked at me. "You've fifteen men, I think."

He was right, of course. If the boys insisted upon backing Tom there would be a slaughter. The town would suffer, but our boys would be shot to doll rags.

"I'll see what I can do."

The bartender watched me leave, and I could see the worry on the man's face. He had a family here, and when shooting started there was no telling who might get hurt.

Out on the street, I stood for a minute in the sunlight. There was only one thing to it, of course. I'd have to pull the crew out of town. We'd have to move the herd.

Kate was at the hotel when I walked in, and I knew she had heard something. We went to a quiet corner of the big, almost empty lobby and sat down.

"What did he say?"

"No give to him, Kate, but I see his point. He doesn't dare open the door even a crack." And then I told her what John Blake had said about Linda McDonald.

"It doesn't make sense to me, Kate. Why would a girl do a thing like that?"

Kate was silent, and I waited; for Kate, despite all her surface hardness, was an understanding woman with a lot of savvy where people were concerned.

"She may hate men . . . and she may love her father."

"I don't get you."

"Sometimes, often without knowing it, a girl measures all men by her father. She may enjoy seeing him run them off, and to her it may be a way of continually proving her father's superiority."

"Kate, how do we stand with Hardeman?"

"He's offered twenty-two dollars a head, but I think he'll go to twenty-five."

"Take it, Kate. Let's get out of here."

She looked at me quickly. "Is it that bad?"

"I've told him I'd back Tom. That means that if Tom goes the other side of the street, I'll be going with him."

"And you'd fight Blake?"

"It may come to that."

She got to her feet. "I'll see Hardeman."

She turned to go, then stopped. "Tom will listen to you, Conn. See him. Tell him how foolish this all is."

"All right."

As I walked along the street I realized how serious it had become. It was much more than a boy going uptown to see a girl, for there was bad blood remaining from the War Between the States. Nine of my boys had fought in the Confederate Army, and most of the others had relatives who had. All of them but one were from Texas. One man . . . and myself.

In a sense, it seemed that I was from Texas, too, for my parents were buried there, and it had been my home longer than anywhere else.

Along the street, in the saloons, the gambling houses, and the stores, and at the livery stable, were men who had fought with the Union, or had been, as I knew McDonald had been, rabid abolitionists. John Blake himself had been a scout for the Union Army.

The Texas trail drivers were, for the most part, uninterested in what lay north of the street. In each trail town there was such a division, and it received unspoken acceptance. The cowhands came to town to have a wild time, and a wild time belonged in the saloons and the houses of the Line. Each man understood that, and regarded it as no slight to be kept south of the street.

John Blake's rule was a reasonable one, and nobody but an occasional belligerent drunk felt called upon to question it. The case of Tom Lundy was something quite different.

Tom was the younger brother of the boss, but he was also the younger brother of every man on the outfit, even those close to his own age. He was a gentleman, and had always conducted himself as one. He rode the wildest of bucking horses, he was a top hand with a rope, he worked right along with the hands and drew the same wages, and while filled with a reckless, devil-take-the-hindmost attitude when in the saddle, he was always a gentleman. He didn't drink, and no man in the outfit would have offered him a drink.

To deny Tom Lundy the right to go north of the street to call on a girl was a direct insult to every man on the Tumbling B.

The bitter feelings left over from the war rankled.

Even in Texas the Davis police force had treated the Texans like second-class citizens, and the resentment burned deep.

John Blake knew what that meant, and he also knew the men of our crew. Every man of them was a veteran of dozens of minor or major gun battles with Indians or outlaws, or of trail-town squabbles. The town might defeat them, might even wipe them out, but other men would die before that happened.

Getting up into the saddle, I rode out toward the herd.

Tom saw me, and came riding my way. He was over six feet—as tall as I was, in fact, and he weighed only a bit less. Seeing him come toward me, I felt a sharp pang of regret for the son I'd never have. Sure, I was only thirty-five, but there was only one woman I wanted, and she was the one I could not have.

"Hi, Conn!" He swung his horse alongside mine. "Can't somebody else take over? I want to go to town."

"I can't let you go, Tom."

His face hardened a little. "What's the matter? Are you afraid of John Blake?"

The minute he said it, he was sorry. I could see it in his eyes, but I felt that old tightness inside of me at the word. It was something you did not say to a gun-carrying man in those days, but I was old enough to carry it off . . . or was I?

"I'm not afraid of him, Tom, and you know damned well I'm not. But if you go north of the street tonight somebody's going to get killed."

"Hell, I'm not afraid!"

"I didn't say you were. Nor did I say it would be you who would get killed."

Words were never my way, and I wasn't handy

with them. Somehow I could never dab a loop on the right phrase, though it wasn't as if I hadn't mingled with folks, and hadn't known how to talk.

"Kid, if you go north of the street tonight," I said, "all hell's going to break loose. Believe me, McDonald won't stand for it."

"Aw, Conn! I can slip in there, see that girl, and get away before anybody knows it!"

"She doesn't really want to see you, Tom."

He didn't believe it, of course, and I should have known he wouldn't. She was the girl he wanted, and the idea that she might not want to see him was unthinkable. It was simply not to be believed.

So I laid it on the line to him, talking as reasonably as I could, and told him what John Blake had said.

"I don't believe it."

"Don't say that where John Blake can hear you."

"The hell with him! Everybody's always talking about John Blake! What's he got, four hands or something?"

"He doesn't need four hands, Tom. Take it from me."

He seemed to be seeing me for the first time, and I knew, suddenly, that whatever place I'd had in the respect of Tom Lundy, I had just lost it.

Death is only a word when you are his age; and much as Tom had seen, he had never seen good men die in a dusty street over a trifle. He had fought in Indian battles, but he had never actually seen a gun battle involving someone he knew and liked.

John Blake was a good man doing a necessary job, and I did not want to kill John Blake. Neither did I want to risk being killed over something like this.

"All right," he said impatiently, "you've told me."

"Don't go, Tom. Don't even think of going."

"You think I'm scared?"

There it was again. At his age it meant so much to prove one wasn't scared. I knew how he felt, because it had not been too long since I had known the same thoughts. And to some extent, I still did.

"It isn't only you, Tom. It's the outfit."

"Hell, Conn, we could take this town apart. The Tumbling B could rope and hog-tie this town."

"Tom, you see that man with the beard, the one sweeping off the walk? That's George Darrough. In two years of buffalo hunting he killed over two thousand buffalo. During that time he had seven Indian fights, and before that he fought through the war. The man who is just now walking up to him is one of the finest rifle shots in the West. It's men like them you'd have to fight."

Tom Lundy had nothing to say to that, but his jaw set stubbornly, and I knew what he was thinking. He was proud of our outfit, and we had just brought a herd through rough country, fighting Indians all the way, and shorthanded the last part of it. He did not like to admit that anything was impossible for the Tumbling B.

Also, he feared Linda McDonald would believe him a loud-mouth if he failed to call.

He had no way of judging the buried animosities that lay hidden between the trail crew and the people of the town.

"I don't want to start a fight, Conn," he said. "When have I ever? All I want to do is go see a girl. What's so wrong about that?"

"Nothing . . . nothing at all, except that nobody wants a cattleman north of the street. It's John Blake's job to see that none of them do—no exceptions."

The disgust on his face was obvious, and I didn't

much blame him. But neither did I see any reason to get a few men killed over such a thing.

Finally he said, "Is it all right if I ride with you when you go back? I'd better see her and tell her I'm not coming."

Well, what could I say? I agreed, figuring he would use good judgment, but I was worried as much about some of the others as I was about him. Delgado was in town and he was not hot-headed, but Rule Carson was, and a wrong word could precipitate a gun battle. The whole outfit felt insulted in the person of Tom Lundy, and, in a way, I didn't blame them. But it was up to me, as well as John Blake, to keep the peace.

Kate was waiting for me at the hotel when I got in town. She had closed the deal with Hardeman, and all that remained was to go to the bank and pick up the money.

Hardeman looked at me. "Conn, one thing I must warn you about. I've heard the talk around town— everybody has—and the man who will pay over the money will be Aaron McDonald."

"So?"

"He's a narrow, disagreeable man, but don't think he does not speak for the town. He does."

"We'll be talking business, that's all."

Hardeman glanced over at Tom. "Sorry, boy. If it was my daughter you'd be welcome, but I have no say here. I am a Kansas City man, just doing business here."

Kate had said very little, but I had been keeping an eye on her, and I was worried. Her face was cold, colder than I could ever remember seeing it, unless it was in a bind when we were fighting Apaches or Comanches somewhere. Tom Lundy was more like a son to her than a brother. She had reared him, brought him up almost from babyhood, and she resented his treatment as much as any of the outfit did.

An idea came to me. "Let's go back to that restaurant," I said. "I could do with something to eat. I mean, after we've finished at the bank."

Nobody said anything, and the three of us went across the dusty street to the bank. Glancing up and down the street, I saw men loitering there, men with coats on . . . men who at this time of day would ordinarily not be wearing coats.

Only John Blake himself stood in front of the bank. He turned squarely toward us and scarcely glanced at me, but he lifted his hand to his hat respectfully at Kate Lundy. "Howdy, ma'am. Hope you've had a nice trip up the trail."

"No more trouble than is to be expected at this time of year, Mr. Blake." She looked at him coolly, and then said, "You know, what you told Mr. Dury is correct. We have only fifteen men with us, but by now there are at least twenty other outfits starting north from Texas. And the Clements boys are bringing two herds this year."

The Clements boys had had their share of trouble, and they had coped with it.

John Blake's big head thrust forward. "Now, Mrs. Lundy, there's no call for us to have trouble. You just keep that boy of yours south of the street—"

"Why?" Tom spoke for the first time, keeping his voice low. "Why should I stay south of the street, Mr. Blake? Am I some sort of a savage? Am I an outlaw? By what right do you discriminate against me?"

Tom Lundy had been well taught, and he had read in his books, and when he wished he could talk like it. There was a time when I had spent an hour or two a day with him myself, and in some ways I had a better education than the average man of my time, although my schooling had been short.

Kate had spent a lot of time with Tom, more time than I had, teaching him to act the gentleman. She knew how it should be, but those months in England and on the Continent that I'd put behind me, they helped. No man had had a stranger life than mine, although the West was filled with men from everywhere, from all countries and all walks of life, and often the walks have been very varied, owing to the kind of men we were.

John Blake was baffled and worried. He looked at Tom Lundy, and I could see the doubt in his face. John Blake understood tough cowhands, tracklayers and gamblers, and he knew how to handle them, but Tom Lundy was a nice boy, and Blake recognized him as one.

"I did not make the law," Blake said.

"Is it law?"

"It's a local ordinance," Blake insisted, "and I enforce it. No Texas men north of the street."

Tom Lundy stood with his feet close together. He stood very straight and he said politely, "Mr. Blake, Conn Dury has spoken of you, and I have nothing but respect for you and for your rules. Nevertheless, I shall be north of the street tonight. You may expect me."

Well, sir, mad as I was at the boy, I couldn't but admire him; and catching a glimpse of John Blake's startled eyes as we turned away, I knew that John did, too.

At the bank door, Tom turned back. "Mr. Blake, what I shall do tonight, I shall do alone, and when I come across the street, I shall come alone. I shall come without Conn, without the Tumbling B."

We went inside and walked up to the railing where
Dick Hardeman waited for us. His face was pale,
and I thought he looked angry. And then I looked
beyond him at the man behind the rolltop desk, and
I understood why.

Aaron McDonald was a narrow-built man, high-
shouldered and thin, a dry-as-dust man, and he
seemed fleshless. His eyes were deep-set under bushy
brows, his cheeks were hollow. He glanced from me
to Kate, nodded briefly, then opened a drawer and
took out a sack of gold and began counting out the
money. Kate had settled at twenty-three dollars per
head; it was a nice lot of gold money, and Aaron
McDonald was a man who respected money.

He watched me put the gold and greenbacks into a
sack for Kate, and then he said, "Your business here
is finished?"

"I've some calls to make," Tom said quietly.

"You are welcome," McDonald said, "south of the
street."

"Tonight I shall be coming north of the street to
call upon your daughter."

Aaron McDonald lifted his eyes from his ledgers.
They were like ice. "My daughter will not be receiving this evening. You are free to do what business you have; beyond that you are not welcome."

"I shall be calling," Tom replied quietly.

"Mr. McDonald," Hardeman interrupted, "this is a
good lad. I have known Kate Lundy and this boy
for years, and—"

"I am not interested in your opinions, Mr. Hardeman. I trust you are not planning to order the affairs
of my household?" He stood up. "This is a place of
business, and it seems our business has been com-
pleted."

Kate's back was stiff. For the first time in years

Kate Lundy was angry. "Tom, let us go. This is no place for us."

Aaron McDonald was a mean man, and a cruel one, and he could not forego the final word. "That's right," he said. "We put up with your kind south of the street. I hope you will permit us to choose whom we entertain north of it."

I slapped him.

Reaching across the rail, I took him by the scruff of his neck and jerked him bodily toward me, and then I slapped him. My hand is big, it is work-hardened and rough, and I slapped him once, then back-handed him across the mouth.

"When you speak to a lady," I said, "be careful of your language."

Behind me I heard John Blake's voice. "Conn . . . let him go."

I did not turn my head. "Are you holding a gun on me?"

"No . . . I am asking you."

Without a word, I dropped McDonald back into his chair. Turning, I said, "You had better teach him some manners."

McDonald was livid. He leaped from his chair. "You god-damned trash! We should have wiped you all out! We should have gone through the South with fire and burned every house to the ground! By—!"

Suddenly, I was smiling. I rested my two hands on the railing and looked at him, and my smile seemed only to increase his fury. "Mr. McDonald," I said quietly, "it might interest you to know that I was an officer under General Sheridan."

Kate spoke from behind me. "Conn . . . come. *Quickly!*"

Turning sharply, I reached her side in two quick strides. Lounging before the bank were Delgado,

Red Mike, and Rule Carson. Tom Lundy had stepped out to join them.

In a rough half-circle, facing them, holding shotguns and rifles, were nine men of the town.

"Kate," I said, "you stay here, I'll—"

"No," John Blake interrupted, "there'll be no shooting." He stepped past me and went through the door, walking to the curb, where he stood facing the men of the town.

"There will be no shooting here," he said. "Put up your guns."

I took Kate Lundy's arm and we went through the door. Our men around us, I escorted her to her rig, and helped her in. Delgado went to the hitching rail and got our horses, and one by one, facing them across our saddles, we mounted up.

Suddenly I was conscious of Tallcott's eyes, and glanced down. In my left hand I was holding Kate's sack of gold, and it was heavy. The expression in Tallcott's eyes was one that did not appeal to me.

Placing the sack beside Kate in the ambulance, I said, "All right—let's go."

In a tight bunch, we started out of town.

The men still stood in the street, but as we neared the end of the street a man dropped from a roof in plain sight, and then another man led two horses from between the buildings.

Tod Mulloy and Van Kimberly both carried rifles, and from where they had been situated could have covered the street at a range of no more than sixty yards.

Both of them sat their horses, one on either side of the street, rifles in their hands, watching the men around Tallcott. And not a man in that group but now knew they had been sitting ducks for the last ten minutes. It was a feeling no man could relish, and never again would any of them feel quite sure that there was not a hidden rifleman some place close by.

We were almost to the end of the street when I heard Kate's exclamation, and saw Linda McDonald standing alone on the boardwalk. She stood before the hardware store, the last building but one in the town, and she carried a neat little parasol in her hands. She looked up as Tom Lundy drew rein before her.

She was beautiful. Of that there could be no question, and I could not find it in my heart to blame Tom. Surely he had seen no such girl on the lonely ranches where most of our time was spent.

Yet . . . Was I seeing her now through the eyes of John Blake and of Moira? There was something there, a certain coldness, a tightness of feature, something I did not trust.

"Your father told me you were not receiving guests tonight," Tom said quietly.

She looked up at him, a small smile about her lips. "Did *I* say that?"

"No, but—"

"My father is a very hard man," she said, closing her parasol with a sudden, very feminine gesture. "I am not surprised that you are afraid of him."

"I am not afraid of him!" Tom replied shortly. "I just do not want to be where I am not wanted."

"Our house," she said, "still stands among the cottonwoods at the end of the street."

Deliberately, she turned and walked away from him, her shoulders very prim, her hips less so.

Tom turned his horse as if to ride after her, and for the first time he saw me. His cheeks flushed.

"You didn't have to listen!" he said irritably. "What do you take me for?"

"A Texan alone in a town that dislikes Texans," I said quietly. "Look!"

Across the street Tod Mulloy had reined in his horse, and in his hands he held a Winchester.

"I'm sorry," Tom said.

He fell in beside me and, almost reluctantly, Tod followed.

In silence we rode almost to the herd before Tom spoke. "Conn . . . I've got to go over there tonight. I've got to."

The worst of it was, I knew how he felt. I knew how he felt about the girl, and about Aaron Mc-Donald, for McDonald's very attitude was an insult and a challenge.

Over such things the fortunes of men are altered.

As for me, I was old enough and wise enough in such a situation, to ride away, but how could he be, at his age?

And could I have ridden away if it were Kate back there?

CHAPTER 3

Dick Hardeman was at the herd when we arrived, and he had three hands with him. That spelled something to me; it was getting on to dark and a poor time to start moving a herd, but it did give me an estimate of the feeling in town.

"Thought we'd pick up the cattle now, Mrs. Lundy," Hardeman said awkwardly. "No use you having the trouble of them."

"It's that bad, is it?" Trust Kate to see through anything like that.

"Yes, ma'am, it is." Hardeman's face was gloomy. "If I were you I'd move off away from here as soon as ever it's dark . . . and leave a fire going."

"You think they'll come after us?" Tom was incredulous. "Whatever for?"

"Aaron McDonald," Hardeman said dryly, "is a proud man. If he lives to be a hundred he will never forget that cuffing you gave him, Conn. You've made an enemy for life."

"He had it coming."

"I agree." He paused, then he asked, "Was that true? Were you with Sheridan?"

"Sure . . . the boys know it. Ran Priest was a Union man, too. But as far as we're concerned, the war is over."

When they had moved off with the herd, we stood around our fire. Only the remuda was left, that and the chuck wagon and Kate's ambulance.

"We will do as Hardeman suggested," Kate said. "We will move off to that knoll over there. There's a sort of hollow just over the top, and we'll bed down there."

"I'd like to ride in there," Rule Carson said bitterly, "and shoot hell out of the place!"

"That's enough of that," Kate said quietly. "We've had trouble enough for this trip. I don't want to take any more empty saddles back to Texas."

"Nobody's waiting for me," Rule said truculently.

"There's a bunk at the Tumbling B that would miss you, Rule," Kate said, and there were several chuckles, for Carson was a man who liked his sleep.

Red Mike took up a rifle and moved away from the fire to stand watch toward the town. Tod Mulloy and Delgado went toward the horses and bunched them as if for night, lined them up with the knoll so their blackness blended with the shadows of the hill, making them invisible from the town. Then very slowly they drifted the remuda away.

The sun was scarcely down before the two wagons rolled out, and within an hour the move had been accomplished.

"If you ask me," Red Mike said, "that Tallcott was doing a lot of thinking about the gold in that sack, ma'am."

Kate stood over the small fire that we had built, well sheltered from view. "Conn, why don't you let some of the boys sleep right now? There's four hours of good sleep before midnight."

When the three men who were standing the first guard had drifted out to their positions, Kate and I sat over the last coals.

Maybe Tom Lundy hadn't used good judgment in getting himself in a stew over Linda McDonald but, after all, he wasn't the first man to get involved with the wrong woman . . . and no one could deny that she was pretty.

Trouble might have developed without that. When there is so much underlying bad feeling, it takes small reason to start trouble, and in the past some of the Texas boys, sore over the defeat of the South, had been only too ready to start shooting again. And there were always hotheads ready to shoot back.

Men like McDonald, with their precise, narrow way of looking at things, could not know what it meant to a bunch of men, all of them young and full of vinegar, to let off a bit of steam. By the time they'd been three months or so on the trail north, eating the dust of the drag, chasing strays, fighting Indians, stampedes, and ornery broncs, working from before daylight until after dark, they were ready to let go a little.

One time I had heard a cowhand asked what a chuck wagon looked like, and he said, "How would I know? I never saw one in the daylight!"

Moreover, I couldn't find it in me to blame Tom. The good Lord knew I'd done my share in making a fool of myself, and had no patent on the idea, either. If McDonald had just let the thing alone it would probably have all been over by now. As it was, men might die before it was settled.

The night on the plains was a time of quietness. Only a far-off coyote, complaining to the listening stars, caused a faint break in the stillness, and his voice seemed only to make the silence more silent still.

The dull red of the coals were a somber light in their small pocket of heat. From time to time their seeking heat seized upon some overlooked bit of dry wood, and then a tiny blaze would leap up briefly, consuming the wood.

"I'd like us to be moving before daylight," Kate said, "and if we pull out toward the west we can swing wide around the town. That way we can avoid trouble, and we might see something of that country out there."

We sat there, talking quietly, but all the while my ears were straining into the darkness, listening for sounds I hoped not to hear.

"I never knew you were a Union man, Conn," Kate said. "You've never talked much about yourself."

"You've heard enough stories."

"But you never know which ones are true. After all, I know nothing of you except that you were a gunfighter or something. You just came riding up when I needed help, and you stayed. I wouldn't know what to do without you, Conn."

That made me feel the fool. Kate would get along, for there was a resilience in her like fine-tempered steel. She reminded me of a Toledo blade, a rapier I saw once in Spain. She had great strength, but she wasn't rigid . . . like McDonald, for example.

It was she who had built that ranch, built it from the grass roots up, and it had taken some doing. In my way, I'd helped.

"There's little enough to tell about me," I said. "They tell me I was born back on the Rapidan River in Virginia, but my folks moved to Texas. When I was nine the Apaches wiped them out and carried me off into Mexico. For three years I was an Apache, then I stole a pony and rode out of the Sierra Madre and back to Texas."

Pa had walked to the spring for a bucket of water, and I had taken the axe and was hitting a couple of

licks at an old mesquite stump in the yard. It was a
big old thing, and without a stump-puller it would be
a long, hard job getting it out—and there was much
else to do. So Pa left an axe sitting beside it, and any
time one of us passed we worked at cutting the tap
root or other roots to loosen it up.

Ma was inside putting up her hair, for this was
Sunday, and when Pa returned from the spring there
was to be a Bible reading.

It was a fair time for us all, for there'd been little
else but work from the time when Pa first decided to
settle on the creek. On Sundays, though, after the
Bible reading, Pa and Ma would read from one of
the other books we had, and lately I'd taken my turn.

I liked best the poems "Marmion" or "Lochinvar,"
but some of the others were good, too—like "The
Rime of the Ancient Mariner."

All of a sudden Ma called from the house, and there
was something funny about her voice. She said,
"Conn, come in here right away . . . don't argue."

The way she spoke scared me, for it wasn't like Ma
at all, so I turned and started for the house, still
carrying the axe.

Ma had the door open a crack, but the creak of the
window swinging out made me look that way, and it
was just in time to see Pa's rifle thrust through the
window. It went off with a loud *bang* and I turned,
looking for what Ma was shooting at, and then there
was another *bang* and the *whiff* of an arrow . . . and
Ma was dead.

Afterward, learning what I did learn, I was glad it
happened that way. When I broke and ran for the
door it was already too late, and when somebody
came running up behind me I turned and swung with
the axe. It was caught and wrested from my hand, and
I looked up into the face of an Apache.

Hours later, when we were over the border in Mexico and heading for the Sierra Madre, I could see the face of my father as I had last seen it. When they led me away we went past the spring and he was lying there, three arrows in him. One was in his back, the other two in his chest. He had turned and faced whatever it was attacking him, and if he'd had a gun he might have made a pass at defending himself.

Folks had warned him about moving around without a gun, but Pa had never seen a live Indian up to then, and he made light of the danger. That was why, my life long, I never went without a gun.

They drove off fifty head of cattle, some horses, mules, and a few sheep. The sheep they ate right off because they couldn't keep up, and the mules next, because Apaches favor mule meat.

It was a far place in the Sierra Madre where they took me, near the head of the Bavispe River. It was the wildest, most terrible and beautiful place I have ever seen. We climbed trails I wouldn't have expected a squirrel to climb. Here and there a steer slipped off the rim and fell on the jagged rocks far below, but the Apaches paid little attention.

The Bavispe was a cold, clear stream, running down from a virgin forest of pines. It was country that was magnificent in its wildness and grandeur, and there, for three years, I lived like an Apache. And never once did I take my mind from the idea of escape.

Not that I showed it. An old mountain man who had stopped by our place one time said the only way to get along with Indians was to live their life and to be a better Indian than they were. So I pitched right in with them, and after a while they tried to help me.

By the time I was twelve I was a fair tracker, hunter, and trapper, and was a better rider than any Apache I'd seen. They were never horsemen in the way the Kiowas or the Comanches were. And then one day a big war party left on a raid north of the border, and two days after they left I stole a pony and, taking a trail I had discovered while hunting, I lit out.

East was the way I went, deciding they would not expect that.

For two weeks I lived off the country the way the Apaches did, and then I crossed over the Rio Grande, swimming my horse.

Half starved, wearing only a breechclout and a stolen coat much too large for me, and riding a worn-out Indian pony, I rode up to a lonely camp not far from the river. There were three men in that camp, and two of them had guns on me before I could speak. The third man just sat there on the sand and looked at me.

"Apache!" one of the men said. "By the Lord, it's an Apache!"

"Sir," I said, "my name is Conn Dury, and I've been a prisoner."

"All right, old chap," the man on the ground said. "Get down and come up to the fire. There's plenty to eat."

His name was James Sotherton. He was only a few months out of England, but he had a period of army service behind him, with service in India and on the Northern Frontier.

When we had eaten, he got my story from me, and had many questions about the way of life of the Apaches, and by that time only an Apache could have known it better than I did.

"And now what?" he asked.

"I must find work," I said, "and get some clothing."

"And an education, wouldn't you say?"

"Yes, sir."

"Have you no relatives? No friends?"

"None, sir."

"Well, we can take care of the job right here. I'll need help with my stock."

One of the others, a big, dark man with a beard, interrupted. "I'd think about that, Mr. Sotherton. This boy may have escaped, like he claims. Or he may be a spy for them redskins."

"I have thought about it." Sotherton spoke with finality. "You're hired, Conn. Now get some sleep."

The man with the beard was named Morgan Rich, and he was a man I would never forget. Bob Flange was his shadow, and both had hired out to Jim Sotherton in San Antonio.

What inspired Sotherton to take the course he did, I could never guess, but he was headed into the Big Bend country, the wildest country in Texas, which at that date was still seventy-five per cent wild. More than likely it was simply a love of wild country for its own sake that headed him into the Big Bend, but before long I got the impression that Morgan Rich and Bob Flange believed he was riding there for another reason.

It so happened that I knew aplenty about the Big Bend country, for the Indians with whom I had been a prisoner, traveled that route and knew that country. Time and again they had fought the Comanches there, and when the going got rough they always knew how to disappear.

The Apache whose prisoner I was, and who seemed to really like me, had told me a good deal about the Big Bend.

Aside from the pony I rode and a torn piece of blanket, the only thing I had been able to bring away from the camp was a pistol.

It was an almost new gun that I had picked off the

body of a dead Apache after a fight near the Bavispe. He must have taken it off a body during the fight earlier that day, because nobody went around looking for it after he was found dead, as they would have had they known of it.

I had hidden the gun under a rock, and I waited until the time came to make my run for the border; then I recovered it.

The three men and I built a rock hut at the foot of Burro Mesa near a spring, and there we settled down. We built corrals, started a small vegetable garden which it was my job to care for, and hunted wild horses. We caught a few, but most of them were not worth the trouble.

Every now and again we all rode out of there and went to San Antonio. On one of those trips Morgan Rich and Bob Flange quit.

It was after we got back to the ranch that Jim Sotherton started my education.

Somehow or other we got on the subject of poetry and I quoted him some of "Marmion" that I recalled from the readings at home. After that, there was a change.

While I taught him to track and to live off the country like an Apache, he taught me all he could think of about English literature, history, and other subjects. At some time or other he had been an instructor in a military school in England—I think it was Sandhurst—and he knew a good deal about teaching.

We spent a good bit of time riding over the country, and from time to time we went to San Antonio or to Austin, and then one day to New Orleans. There we went to a bank and Sotherton picked up some money, quite a lot of it, in gold.

Then he bought some books and some new equipment, and he bought me a Henry .44 rifle.

It was the day after we got back to the place at the foot of Burro Mesa that I found the tracks—and they were not Apache tracks. Somebody had been around the place while we were gone.

Every man's track is distinctive. A man's trail is as easily recognized as his signature. In my own mind I was sure one of the men whose tracks I saw was Morgan Rich.

When I told Sotherton what I thought he merely nodded and made some comment to the effect that the men had probably come back hunting a job . . . maybe they would show up again.

I felt sure that Rich had thought Sotherton was hunting Spanish treasure . . . gold.

And I found out later that when we came back from New Orleans—where nobody knew we had been—and Jim started spending gold money around, Rich and Flange had heard about it.

"If anything ever happens to me," Sotherton told me one time, "you mail this letter."

He hid the letter behind a loose brick in the wall, and I thought no more about it.

It was shortly after we returned from New Orleans that Sotherton sent me out to check on a water hole to see if wild horses had been drinking there. It was a long ride, and when I got back it was almost night.

There had been three of them this time. Morgan Rich, Bob Flange, and a stranger. And what they had done to Jim Sotherton was worse than Apaches would have done.

They must have had it in their minds that he had found Spanish treasure, and they had tortured him to make him tell . . . which, of course, he could not do.

The gold he had had been taken. His guns were gone, his outfit and mine, as well as the horses.

The way it looked, they had come up shortly after I left, and of a sudden it came over me that they might be still about, so I grabbed up what I could and hightailed it for the hills, where I waited until daybreak. Then I made a wide sweep.

They were gone, all right. They had headed out of the country, toward San Antonio.

I went back to our place, and when I had buried Mr. Sotherton, I followed them. But first I took the letter from its hiding place, and when I reached San Antonio I mailed it.

A few days later I located a man who had seen the three men headed northeast, and I went in the direction they had taken, picking up their trail and holding to it until I came up to their camp on the Leon River.

Only one man was in camp and, leaving my horse tied, I walked up to camp holding my six-shooter in my hand.

When I came through the brush I saw that it was Bob Flange squatting beside a fire with a coffee pot on.

"You killed Mr. Sotherton," I said as I came up behind him.

His shoulders hunched as if I'd hit him with a stick, and then he turned his head around slowly to get a look at me. He got to his feet.

"Now see here, boy," he said, "you don't know what you're talkin' about."

"That's his rifle there. Those are his horses picketed yonder."

He was figuring his chances on going for his gun, and wondering whether he could get into action before I did.

"You murdered him," I said, "and you tortured him.

That gold you stole he got in New Orleans. I was with him there."

"There's a treasure," Flange said insistently. "What else was he doin' down there in that country?"

"He liked wild country," I said. "You killed a man, a good man, with no better reason than a foolish thought that he might know where there was gold."

His manner was growing confident. "What do you figure on doing, boy? If you want some of the gold"— he reached into a shirt pocket and took out a bright gold piece—"you can have this." He spun the gold coin into the dust.

Like a fool, I looked down at it, and he drew and shot at me. Only he was in too much of a hurry, and he missed . . . I didn't.

I picked up that gold piece and took whatever else of gold was in his pockets, because it wasn't rightfully his and I might need it to trace the other men. Whatever was left I would send to Mr. Sotherton's folks in England.

Then I took the horses and rode in to the Fort and went to the commanding officer. He looked up from his desk when the corporal showed me in.

"What can I do for you, young man?"

"My name is Conn Dury," I said, "and three men murdered my boss." And then I told him the whole story. I ended it by saying, "I came up with one of them this morning. He's in his camp down on the Leon River."

"We will go get him," the captain said.

"No need to take anything down there but shovels," I said. "I already saw him."

He looked at me very carefully, and then said, "And the other two?"

"I'm setting after them." From my pocket I took three hundred dollars in gold. "This is stolen gold. It was in his pockets. I also brought in ten head of stolen horses that belonged to Mr. Sotherton. I figured you might send this gold back to his family in England, and dispose of the horses for them."

He sat back in his chair and looked at me. "How old are you, son?"

"Fifteen," I said, "but I've been doing a man's work."

"So I see." From the pile of gold he counted out sixty dollars. "You will need some money if you expect to follow those men. You realize, of course, they will try to kill you?"

"Yes, sir. But Mr. Sotherton treated me well. He paid me, gave me as much education as we had time for, and no man should be treated as they treated him."

Captain Edwards rose from his desk and walked outside with me. "You have that address?"

"Yes, sir." I handed it to him.

He glanced at it, then looked at it again, and something about it seemed to surprise him.

"I see," he said. "So that is who your Mr. Sotherton was . . . James Sotherton . . . Major James Sotherton." He studied the address. "A very distinguished man, my boy, from a very distinguished family."

We walked to the corral where I had left the horses and he selected two of them, after a glance at my own horse. They were the two finest of the lot. "You take those horses," he said. "I will give you a letter showing right of possession."

He also gave me the weapons I had brought in from Flange's camp. "I shall write to his family," Captain Edwards said. Then he went on, "Did he ever mention his family? Or anyone else?"

"Never, sir."

"Let me know what happens." The captain hesitated a moment, and then he said, "This is a remarkable coincidence. As a young officer I knew your Major Sotherton. He was a military attaché during the war with Mexico."

Two weeks later I found out who the third man was. He was Frank Hastings . . . a scalp hunter . . . a man whom I had never seen.

When I came on Morgan Rich it was in Las Vegas, New Mexico, more than six months later.

He was in a saloon there, and I walked up to the bar near him and said bluntly, "You murdered Jim Sotherton. You tortured him worse than any Apache."

"You lie!" he shouted at me.

But at least twenty men were listening, and he looked worried.

"You stole gold money from him, and left a trail of it clear across the country. It was English gold."

Nobody was doing anything but listening as I went on. "I traced Bob Flange by it, too."

"Flange?"

"He missed his first shot . . . I didn't."

"Get out of here, kid. You're crazy."

"That belt you have on," I said steadily, "is a British uniform belt you stole from his outfit after you killed him."

"You're a damned liar!" Rich said hoarsely, and as he spoke he drew his gun.

It was cold out on the hill the next morning, with a raw wind blowing, so they buried him in a shallow grave, wrapped in his blanket, then hurried back to the saloon for a drink.

Frank Hastings had dropped from sight, and I had never found him.

The coals were almost gone. "You'd best get some sleep, Kate," I said. "It is going to be a long night."

She was getting to her feet when we heard the

shots. A sudden volley . . . and then one more. The shots came from the town.

Kate turned sharply to me. "Conn . . . where's Tom?"

Fear tore my throat like a rasp. I turned and ran in a stumbling gait toward the place where the men had bedded down. Tom's bedroll was there, and it was empty.

Priest rolled over and lifted himself on one elbow. "What's wrong? What's happened?"

"Tom's gone," I said, "and there was shooting in town."

His horse was gone, too. When I returned from checking the remuda, everybody was up and armed.

And then we heard the galloping of horses out on the prairie. The riders drew up well out in the darkness, at least a hundred yards off.

There was a thump of something thrown to the ground, and a voice shouted, "And don't come back!"

They rode off quickly into the darkness, and we went out there. Bending down, I lit a match.

It was Tom Lundy, and he was dead. He had been shot three times in the back, and then somebody had turned him over and shot him between the eyes from such close range that the wound was marked with powder burns.

We carried him back to the hill and laid him down on the ground, and Kate Lundy came and stood over him.

He was her last living relative, and he had been both brother and son to her. After her husband had been killed by Indians Tom was all she had left, and now he was gone.

His gun was in its holster, the thong still in place, evidence that he had not expected shooting trouble. Standing there, we looked down at those bullet holes. Three shots in the back at close range that had ripped through his back, tearing great holes through his chest. And in case he was still not dead, a man had leaned over him and finished the job with a pistol bullet.

Suddenly Red Mike began to swear in a choked, horrible voice.

Tod Mulloy said, "If it's the last thing I do, I'm going to burn that town."

"Let's do it now," Carson said. "Right now!"

"No."

The word was flat, cold, in a voice such as I had never heard Kate Lundy use before.

"No," she repeated.

"We're pulling out?"

"No."

That was all she would say, and the men were silent.

Nobody slept that night, but in the morning Naylor and Priest went out and dug a grave on a flat place at the very top of the hill. They dug it deep, and we buried Tom Lundy there.

Looking off toward town, using the field glasses I kept in my saddlebag, I could see the glint of rifles from the rooftops or corrals.

"They're waiting for us, Kate," I said. "They are waiting to get us as we ride in."

"We're not going in."

Rule Carson swore. "Now, look here, Mrs. Lundy," he began. "Tom was—"

"Tom Lundy," she said, "was my brother. He took my husband's name, and my husband considered him his son." She paused. "We wanted children, but we never had any . . . only Tom."

She turned to Red Mike. "Mike, I want you to saddle the steel-dust, and I want you to ride to Texas. I want you to find twenty-five men who can handle guns, and who can take orders." She looked over at the town. "Can you find that many?"

"I can find a hundred," he said. "Volunteers, if you want them."

"I want men who work for wages," she said, "and I've the money to pay them."

Red Mike turned to look at me. "Who do you think?" he asked.

"The Cuddy boys," I said, "and Harvey Nugent, Sharkey, Madden, and Kiel. Some of the Barrickman or Clements boys if they're around."

Kate stood there, looking toward the town, a tall, lonely woman, with high cheekbones and a face still lovely despite what sun and wind had done to it.

"You're going to fight, Kate?"

"Not the way they expect," she said. "Not at all the way they expect."

But it was that morning that it began, and it was a kind of warfare I had not expected, and was not prepared for. Nor were they.

She wrote three telegrams that morning, and she sent Delgado off on a fast horse to take them to the nearest station to the east. It was a water tank and saloon twenty miles away.

The day drifted slowly by and the men sat around playing cards. Toward sundown they drifted the horses to the nearest creek and watered them.

Riflemen still stood guard on rooftops and in the alleys approaching the town.

Kate remained in her ambulance most of the day, and the rest of us waited.

"They must be getting kind of nervous down there," Tod Mulloy said finally. "We've got the edge, because we know what we're doin' and they don't."

The thought seemed to cheer everybody up a little,

and I noticed that every once in a while one of the men would go up the rise and stand there looking off toward the town. They could see us up there, and our inaction must be puzzling to them.

"They will not sleep much tonight," D'Artaguette commented. "Nor did they last night."

Kate looked over at him. "Nor will they for many nights to come."

At noon on the third day, a rider came toward us bearing a white flag. With my field glasses I could see it was Bannion, the one man in town—unless it was Hardeman—who might be allowed close enough to talk.

Bannion had always been fair. He had staked more than one busted trail hand to a final drink when his money was gone, and had even furnished a couple of riders with horses to get back to their outfits.

Kate, D'Artaguette, and I went down the slope to meet him.

"I had nothing to do with this, Mrs. Lundy," he said. "I want you and the boys to know that. Nothing at all. I didn't even know it was going to happen."

"Did they ask you to come out and look the situation over?" I asked.

"Yes . . . they're worried. They can't figure what's happening. They've been laying for you, expecting an attack just any minute."

"Let them worry," Kate replied. "Mr. Bannion, you have the reputation for being a fair man. Now we're going to give you a chance to save yourself. You will have no time to consider this, but take my advice and do as I say.

"Go back to town. Tell them the truth, that we would not allow you into our camp. Then sell your saloon."

"Sell my saloon?" he repeated in astonishment.

"Why, I can't do that! Anyway, they would think it mighty odd—"

"Would you rather sell at a loss—and you may have to—or come out with nothing at all?"

"What do you mean by that?"

"Mr. Bannion," Kate asked quietly, "did you ever see a town die?"

He just looked at her, and after a minute he said, "Thank you, ma'am. Thank you." Then he turned his horse.

"Mr. Bannion," Kate added, "and this is for you, and you alone to know. One hundred miles west of here there's a creek that flows along the edge of a wide flat. There are hills to the north, and some cottonwoods there. It's on the main line of the railroad."

Well, I looked at her. Of course, I knew the place; we had camped there once. In fact, I myself had camped there several times, and had taken our herd there the season before.

What she had in her mind I did not know, but looking at her face—and never had I seen it so cold —I knew what was going to happen to the town.

That town, the town that had killed her brother, was going to die.

It was not a man, nor several men who were going to die, but the town itself.

CHAPTER 4

Kate Lundy had given no instructions to Red Mike other than to hire fighting men, but we all knew that Red Mike would tell the story of what had happened. And it was such a tale as would be carried by the winds and the dust until it was the talk of every campfire and every ranch house in all of Texas.

We camped on the knoll under the Kansas sky, and we let the days drift by, but there was plenty to do. On the fourth day two riders drifted toward our camp, and both of them I knew.

They were fighting men encountered en route by Red Mike and sent on to us. Bledsoe was a former Ranger who had served with Big-Foot Wallace, and Meharry was a tough young Irishman who had fought in the French army at Sedan, a veteran soldier.

Priest and Naylor she sent off to the west to the place she had spoken of to Bannion, and they had their instructions. When she took them aside and told them what they were to do, they just looked at her, then at each other. Suddenly, both started to grin; and they were still grinning when they rode off to the west.

"Conn," Kate said to me, "mount the men, and just at dusk ride toward the town."

I waited. There were men with rifles waiting there

in town, under cover. We would be riding up in the open.

"Ride until you are just out of rifle shot," Kate said, "and make sure you give yourself the benefit of the doubt; then ride around the town. Do not come back until after dark."

Smart . . . she would have them alerted once more, all the night through. It was one more step in a kind of warfare that I'd never have thought of myself, but one look at Kate Lundy told me this was a different Kate. She was fighting . . . fighting to destroy the town that had killed her brother.

Would they finally move out to attack us? If so, we were pitifully few.

That, no doubt, would come. But not just yet. None-theless, when I mounted up to ride out that evening I made sure each man carried fifty rounds of ammunition. Kate remained on the knoll alone . . . but they could not know that . . . or could they?

We started out, riding around the hill in a tight bunch, but shifting around so that our dust made it difficult for them to estimate our number. We rode toward the town, keeping out of rifle range, then swung around it, taking advantage of the terrain to dip into valleys, then to emerge, to keep them guessing as to our intentions. We were on the far side of the town when it became completely dark, and at once we swung around and returned to our camp.

Kate challenged us as we drew near, and when I replied, we rode on in. Later that night she sent Meharry out to start a small campfire on a hill east of town, and to keep it burning for a while.

By now other herds should have appeared, but none came.

The days grew warmer. At night the coyotes howled. On the seventh day the train stopped a mile out of town and let a man out, and let a horse down from a flatcar. It was Delgado, coming back with replies to Kate's messages.

After he had started across country toward us the train went on into town.

The following day a dust cloud appeared to the south of the town, and a big herd of steers showed up. They went to a hollow among the low hills, and an hour later we saw two riders approaching.

One of them was Matt Pollock, who lived a hundred miles east of the Tumbling B. He was a square, powerful man with a quick, energetic way about him. As he rode up to camp we saw that the rider beside him was a man whom we also knew. It was Harvey Nugent, one of the men Red Mike had been looking for.

Pollock swung down and thrust out his hand to Kate. "Howdy, Mrs. Lundy! Hear you're in trouble."

Briefly Kate recounted the story, mentioning the attitude of the town toward Texans. Take their money and get rid of them—that was the town's motto.

"What do you want me to do? Stampede my herd through their cracker-box town? Or burn it around their ears?"

"East of here," Kate explained, "a train will be unloading barbed wire. I have leased the railroad land on both sides of the tracks, and I'm going to fence the town in."

"What about the even-numbered sections? As I understand it, the railroad was granted only the odd-numbered sections."

"Not here, nor at several other points where there was an overlapping of grants for railroad building. I've leased it all at fifty cents an acre."

"You're fencing in the whole town?" Matt Pollock reached for the coffeepot. "Damn it, Kate, you've got to give them an easement! They've got a legal right to go in and out."

"Of course they have. There will be the railroad and a driving road right alongside, and I shall stop nobody from going in or out—except the trail herds. No trail herd can cross my land."

Squatting beside the fire, I watched Kate. I was curious, and a little shocked. Ours was a hard land, and it needed hard people to survive in it, but I had never seen that look on Kate Lundy's face before, except once.

That time was the morning after the Apaches had killed her husband, ran off their stock, and burned their outfit—the morning after I showed up.

When I came down out of the rocks at the end of the attack that I had helped to fend off, she was standing there, hands hanging, her face twisted in that strange, dry grief that was so characteristic of her.

I was to learn that she rarely cried; only her face seemed to go through the motions, but almost without tears, as if long ago she had shed all the tears she had to shed.

She stood there looking down at the crumpled body of her husband, and then the boy came out of the rocks and put his arm around her.

My horse was walking slowly, and I drew up opposite them, but it was several minutes before she looked up. "Thank you," she said simply.

"Ma'am," I said, "I'm sorry. Wish I'd come along sooner."

"There was no warning. They just came out of the desert like ghosts."

"They were Apaches, ma'am. There's never any warning. They'll be all around you before you can make a move."

I got down from the saddle and went around the place, sizing it up. The site was not bad. The spring beside which they had settled was a good one, and they had managed to irrigate enough to start a small vegetable garden. Also they had been clearing away rock to make land for a field.

The house had been built of native stone for the lower courses, and of timbers cut out of driftwood logs snaked up from the river for the upper part. The roof had been made of branches, brush, and earth, but the Apaches' fire had destroyed it, and charred the big timbers. Some of them still smoldered, and I got right at it putting out the fires.

Lundy's rifle was lying where it had fallen, and there were a couple of empty shells on the ground nearby.

He was a man of perhaps thirty-odd, with good features, maybe a trifle over-refined for this country. His hands showed evidence of hard work, but indicated this might have been the first such work he had done. His boots were good—the best, in fact. The same was true of his hat and belt.

Going through his pockets, I took out a couple of gold coins and some odd bits of change. These I placed on a rock with whatever else there was, and then I took the shovel and walked up to a small knoll where there was a mesquite tree growing, gnarled and ancient. There I dug the grave.

It puzzled me why they had come to such a place, for it was far west of any regular settlements and was in an area known to be traveled both by Apaches and Comanches. Not to say it didn't have a certain strange, wild beauty.

"When morning comes," I said, "we will start for San Antonio. You and the boy can ride the horse. I'll walk."

She didn't say anything at all, nor did she say much when I wrapped her husband in an old piece of blanket I found and lowered him into the grave, the boy helping. When I'd filled it in, I said some lines from the Good Book that I recalled—I'd buried a few men before this. Then I found a good place where there was soft sand for them to bed down for the night.

I had no certainty the Apaches would not return at first light, so, dog-tired as I was, I caught a nap, with the boy watching. When daybreak came, I was waiting, but the Apaches evidently figured their medicine was bad, for they didn't show up.

When Kate Lundy awakened I had a fire going and some coffee made. I said to her, "Better drink up, ma'am. It's a long way, and the sooner we start the sooner we will get there."

She stood up and shook out her dress and smoothed it down a mite, and then she looked all around. She looked at the ruins of her house, at the grave of her husband, and at the few, pitifully few things that belonged to them, and then, with that strange, hard expression on her face, she said, "I am not going."

"Ma'am?"

"We're going to stay. This was where we came to settle, and this is where we will settle. We are not going away. Thank you, Mr. Dury, for all you have done."

And that was how I met Kate and Tom Lundy, and how I came to stay with them.

Sitting there across the fire from Kate, I could not but wonder what they were thinking of down in the town. By now there had been time for second thoughts, for taking stock.

They had murdered a fine young man who was

simply going to call on a girl. True, he was breaking the local rule by crossing the street, or rather, by going north of it. But he had done no harm to anyone, nor planned any.

Moira, the waitress in the restaurant, knew what sort of girl Linda McDonald was. So did John Blake. And others must know. They also knew what kind of man Aaron McDonald was.

They knew what they had done, and they had expected an attack with violence, and it had not come. Neither had we gone away.

The column of faint smoke that marked our fire and the white wagon-tops were in plain view of the town, and this would not permit them to forget what had happened. Nor would it allow them to keep from wondering what we planned to do.

For a week the town must have been an armed camp, ready to resist an attack, and the longer we held off the more worried they would become, and the more on edge. Business must be at a standstill down there, for there is a limit to the amount of business a town of that small size can do with itself.

Only one other herd had appeared, and by now they must be aware that they were to have no business from it.

What were they thinking down there? What did they plan? What were they expecting?

On the morning of the eighth day we saw two wagons rolling out of town, headed westward. Kate borrowed my glasses and studied them carefully. Then she returned them to me. "Bannion," she said. "He's moving out."

We saw several people standing in the street watching him go.

Matt Pollock sent his herd off to the west under half a crew. He kept the rest to lend us a hand, but he went with his cattle. He had left us a few beeves, and I killed a buffalo, so we had enough meat.

On the morning of the tenth day the first wagons arrived. One of them was filled with supplies—food, and a thousand rounds of ammunition.

There were three big freight wagons loaded with barbed wire and posts. One wagon went along dropping posts, and when the post holes were dug and the posts in place, a team pulled one end of the barbed wire out along the posts and the men followed with wire-stretchers and hammers. Eight or ten men with a couple of teams of horses and unbroken prairie on which to work can string a lot of wire.

And through the day they were watching us from the town.

It was mid-afternoon before John Blake rode out from town.

He rode a handsome black horse and he was dressed in his black broadcloth suit. He rode out and sat watching for a few minutes, missing nothing . . . and nobody.

Harvey Nugent was there, a professional fighting man who had fought through three Texas feuds and a dozen brushes with Indians. He was a gunfighter, and his reputation was known to John Blake.

"Howdy, John!" Nugent said cheerfully. "Heard you were around."

"I never expected to see you throwing up fence, Harvey. What is this, anyway? A drift fence?"

Harvey gave him a slow grin. "John, you chose the wrong town this time. This here fence is on land Mrs. Lundy has leased from the railroad."

John Blake studied the fence, and he needed to ask no more questions. He turned his horse and rode up the hill to Kate's ambulance.

We'd rigged a sunshade of canvas for her, and she was sitting under that, watching the work.

"There's coffee on the fire, John," I said. "'Light an' set.'"

He swung down and stood looking at the fence. "I suppose I don't have to ask if you have leased land on the other side of town?"

"Now, just one side wouldn't make much sense, would it? No, we've leased it on both sides, John. East and west, too."

"You can't bottle up a town like that," he protested.

"Bottle up a town?" My voice indicated astonishment. "Why, who would do such a thing? Anybody can leave who wants to go."

Putting down my cup, I added, "In fact, John, I was going to talk to you about that. There's a new town—name of Hackamore—going up out west of here. They'll be needing a marshal. Why don't you look into it?"

"West?"

"Well . . . west and south. A bit closer to the herds coming up from Texas, and there's good holding ground and good water there."

"So that's it."

"That's it, John."

He glanced at Kate from the corners of his eyes, but Kate just sat there, watching the stringing of the wire.

"Ma'am?" he said. "Mrs. Lundy?"

"Yes?"

"I had nothing to do with that, ma'am, nothing at all. I made the rule, but I would never have drawn a gun on that boy."

"I know it, John."

"Are you going to strangle that town, ma'am?

There's good folks down there. Not all of them, but some."

"They killed my brother."

"That was Aaron McDonald and that crowd of blue noses, ma'am. What of the others?"

"They can pull out. The road is open, and they were moving when they came here. As far as that goes, our town is in a better location, with better water than this place."

"You are a hard woman, ma'am."

Kate turned her eyes on him. "Am I, John? That boy was my brother. He was almost a son to me, and my husband adopted him as his son, and Tom took my husband's name. He was all I had in the world, John Blake, and they took him from me. They shot him down in the street. Your town does not deserve to live, and it shall not."

He got slowly to his feet. "They'll fight, ma'am. They'll drive you from the country . . . or bury you."

"I do not think so," Kate replied. "This is leased land. I have every right to be here, every right to fence the land. I am not denying anyone the right to enter or leave—but I will not have trail herds crossing my property."

"And the town was built to supply trail herds. They need the herds to live."

Kate smiled. "Well, Mr. Blake, I am glad to hear you say that. I was wondering when they would come to understand that fact—a fact, I might add, they were apparently not thinking of when they killed my brother. A fact Aaron McDonald was not thinking of when he made his remarks about Texans."

John Blake's face was grim.

"There's another point you might mention, John," I suggested. "You spoke to Harvey Nugent. Now, you know Harvey, and so do I; but those people down

there may not know him. You should tell them about
him.

"If you'll notice, I've got Meharry and Bledsoe here,
too, and Red Mike has gone down the trail to Texas
after two dozen more. We're expecting trouble, John,
and we'll be ready for it. Not asking for it . . . just
ready."

Blake turned sharply around, his big head thrust
forward, his face tight with anger. "You bring that
crowd in here, you turn that bunch loose, and this
will be the bloodiest grass in Kansas!"

Me, I was remembering Tom Lundy, so young, so
proud, his bravery challenged, so unable to believe
that he could die over such a thing.

"John," I said, "there are peoples who believe that
when a young chief dies he should go into the after
world with the skulls of a hundred enemies to mark
his passing. I never cottoned to such ideas, but you
tell those folks down there they can sit right where
they are, or they can move out; but if they move
against that wire they will be met with rifles."

He turned his horse and walked him away down
the hill.

After a moment, Kate said, "Conn, will they come
against us? Will they?"

"Yes, Kate," I said, "they'll come."

CHAPTER 5

So we took up our rifles and patrolled the fence and waited for trouble to come. For now the spur was on the other boot, and it was we who felt the rowel of waiting, waiting for our enemies to come and not knowing when to expect them.

But we were men seasoned by years of trouble, men who had known little else from boyhood on. We were men who had fought wild cattle and wilder horses, who had lived by the gun, and each of us more than half expected to die by gun or stampede or flood.

As the days passed, other men rode in. There was Rowdy Lynch from the Live Oak country, and Teague from the Palo Pinto. Gallardo came from Del Rio, and Battery Mason from Cow House Creek. They drifted into camp by twos and threes and bedded down on the knoll, and when another day came they took their turn at riding fence, the lean, hard men of our Winchester brigade.

On the fifteenth day a train went through, a train of empty cattle cars, bound west for Hackamore, the town we had started in the bend of the river. From our knoll we could see the people come down to the station to meet the train, only to see it breeze on through.

When the next day came, two wagons rolled out of town.

With Kate riding beside me, D'Artaguette, Meharry, Nugent, and I rode down to cut them off. Only one thing we wanted to know—was anybody riding in those wagons who had been among those who killed Tom Lundy.

The man in the first wagon who held the lines did not move to pick up a weapon, for he was a wise man, and he knew that the tempers of men at such a time are on hair triggers.

"You've played hell," he said, looking up at Kate, and then at me.

"My brother was killed."

"Yes, and I don't hold with that." There was genuine sympathy in his eyes. "You've my regrets, for whatever they are worth. I knew Tom Lundy . . . he traded in my store, and was a gentleman, but I said my say back there, and no thanks did I receive for it."

"Drive to Hackamore," Kate said, "and tell Priest I said to show you a site for your store."

"Thank you." He made no move to drive on. And then he said hesitatingly, "I guess we'll be going on."

His wife thrust her head from the wagon. "You tell them!" she said. "You tell them or I will! They've got a lot of men coming in on the train," she went on, "and they're going to wipe you out."

"Who's paying for them?" I asked.

"McDonald and Shalett," the driver answered. "They're putting up most of the money."

"Shalett? I don't believe I know him."

"He knows you. He ran the Prairie Dog—that saloon next to the bank." The man was curious. "I'd say he knew you mighty well, sometime or other. It was his idea to bring in fighters, and he backed McDonald in everything he did."

"Shalett?"

"Frank Shalett. A big, dark man . . . talks mighty little. Funny thing, him and McDonald getting together now. McDonald was all for running him out of town before he'd been there three months. Shalett had killed a man in a gun battle. He killed Port Rader."

The wagons rolled on, and we let them go.

But Harvey Nugent spoke up. "I knew Port," he said, "and he was a good man with a gun. Whoever this Frank Shalett is, he's no tenderfoot."

Port Rader, like Nugent, had been a man for hire, a professional fighting man, brought in to fight rustlers, Indians, or nesters, and a tough man.

But I could remember no Frank Shalett.

No doubt I had forgotten much during the years I was away, traveling in Europe. When a man leaves behind all he knows and remembers, he tends to forget it, and there for a time I had left it all behind.

The year I killed Morgan Rich was the year I was sixteen. It was 1855.

When a boy is foot-loose and drifting, there's no telling where he's apt to end up, and about that time I was walking along the street in Santa Fe one day when I ran into Captain Edwards, the man to whom I had taken Jim Sotherton's possessions after he was murdered.

He caught my arm. "Dury, isn't it? Conn Dury?"

"Yes, sir. And you'll be Captain Edwards."

"You know, Dury, I've a letter for you. I wrote to Sotherton's family, and told them about you, and about the education you had been getting from their son. They want you to write to them."

We walked along to his quarters to get the letter. After he had given it to me, he asked, "You said something about hunting those other men. Did you find them?"

"I found Morgan Rich. He's buried over at Las Vegas."

"And the other one?"

"Hastings . . . he dropped out of sight—probably some Indian killed him. There's a lot of ways a man can die out here. Many such men nobody will ever know about."

"Dury," Edwards said suddenly, "stay and have dinner with me. I am in command here, and the food is good. It will be a pleasure to have you."

He was full of questions at first about the means I'd used to hunt down Rich. Finally we got around to talking about Sir Walter Scott and some of the other writers whose works I'd read, but it seemed to me there was something else on his mind.

After a time, while we were sitting over coffee, he said, "You know, Conn, I don't know all that is in that letter to you, but I do know part of it. They want you to come to England."

At first I was not sure I'd heard him correctly, but then he explained. They had written him that they had the idea they should give me a chance to continue the education their son had begun, and they would, if I wished, send me to school over there, providing tutors to bring me up to date, and whatever was necessary to enter.

"I think," Edwards said, "it is in good part because they want to hear about Jim Sotherton. The things he said, the way he looked, all you can tell them about him. They would pay your way over and back, and your expenses."

He looked at me thoughtfully. "It is a rare opportunity, Conn."

So I went to England.

At the last, Edwards warned me. "Be careful, Conn, about what you say. Remember they are no longer young, and they live in a country that has been civilized for hundreds of years. They are like the people who will come after us here; and when they hear of the West as it really is, they will not believe it.

"They are used to curbstones, and to officers that one can simply call on to take care of malefactors. There is no place in their thinking for a land where a man carries the law in his holster. What I mean is, I wouldn't tell them about Flange and Rich."

In England, they met me at the station, a tall, fine-looking old man with white hair and the erect carriage of a military past, and a girl perhaps a year younger than I.

What they expected I do not know. Possibly they believed I would step down from the train in buckskins and a sombrero; but whatever it was, I do not believe it was what they saw.

Although I was only sixteen, I was more than six feet tall, slim but strong. A friend of Captain Edwards had come down from West Point to help me choose the proper outfit, so there was nothing strange in my appearance, and the only way they could have known me was by my age and the darkness of my skin, browned by Texas sun and wind.

The girl knew me at once, and came to me, her hand outstretched. "You must be Conn Dury. I am Felicia Kirkstone—James Sotherton was my uncle."

She was pretty, and pretty in a way I vaguely remembered from the years before my folks moved west.

"How do you do?" I said. "Mr. Sotherton told me about you."

"Conn . . . Mr. Dury . . . my grandfather, Sir Richard Sotherton."

We talked a little of my crossing, which had been a wild one, due to the terrible storms of that year, and we walked to the open carriage that waited for us. Sir Richard drove, and we rode the short distance to Sotherton Manor behind a handsome pair of blacks.

When the trip had been planned I was uneasy about it, for all I knew had been taught me by Jim Sotherton, aside from my earlier training at home; and I had never traveled.

Sotherton Manor was a large, rambling old house of gray stone, half covered with vines. There was a wide stretch of lawn in front and a winding gravel drive that led to the door. It was far more grand than any place I had ever seen before.

They asked me about my own country, the country where I had worked for Jim; and looking around me, I wondered how I could make them understand. Everything around me indicated that this was a long settled land—the spreading lawns, the carefully planted trees, the green well-kept beauty of it all. Even the woodlands had definite borders, for this was a land where everything had been decided long, long ago.

Here there was custom, tradition, and a common law built upon hundreds of years of living on the same ground, in somewhat the same way. And my land in the Big Bend of the Rio Grande was still wild, untamed. Nothing there was ordered and arranged, nor were there customs or traditions. Everything was raw and new, and the laws were the laws of the sun and the water holes, the wind and the sparse grazing.

But that evening, after dinner, I tried to tell them.

"When Jim Sotherton rode into the Big Bend," I said, "there weren't twenty men in the whole area, and most of them gathered at the old Presidio, a place they called Fort Leaton, down on the Rio Grande."

"How big an area is it?" Sir Richard asked.

"The Big Bend? I don't actually know, but it is larger than Wales . . . perhaps a third the size of Ireland. And this is only a small piece of Texas."

They did not believe me. I could see the doubt in their eyes, and knew it was a poor way to begin our acquaintance, though it was the truth. And I had promised to tell them.

"It's wild, lonely country. Almost everything that grows there has a thorn. The mountains are rugged, bare rock, the country is desolate, yet beautiful— beautiful in a way you'd have to see to understand. There's wild horses, wild cattle, mountain lions, wolves, and rattlesnakes. There are deer, antelope, and javelinas."

"What?"

"Javelinas—wild pigs."

"My uncle told us you had lived with the Apaches," the girl said.

"Yes, ma'am. For most of three years."

Gradually, I began to realize that Mr. Sotherton had written them a good deal about me—about my parents being killed by the Indians, my captivity, and the education he had begun giving me.

Later that night, when we were alone, Sir Richard said, "The men who killed my son . . . they had worked for him, I believe?"

"Yes, sir. They thought he was hunting hidden treasure . . . there are rumors of Spanish treasure in the Big Bend. After he returned from New Orleans and spent some gold money, they came for him. He was dead when I got back to the ranch."

"I see. And the men who killed him? They were apprehended by the law?"

The law? There was no law west of the Pecos, only the long winds and the Comanche Trail.

"They were punished, sir," I answered. "At least, two of the three were punished. The other man is still missing."

For two years I went to school in England, and it was not an easy thing for me, for I had not the habit of study, nor did I know much of books. I did not have the background I needed for this but I struggled, and slowly I learned. Each vacation I spent with the Sothertons, but my thoughts kept straying back to my own wild land.

Often at night I lay awake, smelling the sage brush again, longing for the feel of the cool night wind off the mountain slopes, from over the broken hills, for the sight of Nine Mile Mesa shouldering against the skyline, for the sunlit flanks of the Chisos, for the purple loom of the Carmens across the river in Mexico.

Sometimes when I was studying I would put down my books and stare from the window, remembering a time when I rode up Rough Run to Christmas Spring, or another time when I camped in The Solitario.

At first, I made few friends in the school. There was one, Lawrence Wickes, a boy of my own age but who seemed younger, who had come to the school from India. He was the son of a British army officer stationed on the Northwest Frontier, and when we talked we found we had much in common.

He was with me the day I had my fight.

Most of the boys had been polite, but distant. Nor had I the words to speak with them, for their interests were not mine, and the things we knew were different. The whole world of their conversation concerned topics of which I had no knowledge and with which I had no connection. The people they knew, and the places, these were strange to me, and if occasionally

I blundered into some talk of my own past I would find them looking at me with frank disbelief.

Felicia had told one of the boys that I had been a prisoner of the Apaches, and the story went all over the school. There was one boy—his name was Endicott—who made several slighting remarks about me in my presence.

He was big, and was much thought of as a soccer player and a boxer, and he outweighed me by at least twenty pounds.

"You will have to fight him," Wickes said. "They are saying you are afraid."

"I don't want to, Larry. His father is a friend of Sir Richard's. I might hurt him."

"Hurt *him?*"

"It is a different thing, Larry. He has boxed, and I know nothing of boxing; but I have fought all my life—with Apache boys, with cowhands . . . with men."

"They do not believe anything they have heard of you."

One day, in the presence of others, Endicott told me that I lied. I started to speak, and suddenly, without warning, he struck me.

It was a good enough blow, I suppose. No doubt he intended it to finish me, but he had boxed with boys in school, and I had fought with teamsters, cowhands, and plainsmen. In the West, a boy at fourteen or fifteen did a man's work, and walked in a man's tracks; and when he fought, he fought as a man fights.

Endicott's blow did not stagger me. It caught me on the cheekbone, and when I did not fall, I could see he was shocked. And then we fought.

He knew more of boxing than I, but not a bit of good did it do him, for I plunged in, all the bitterness and savagery within me aroused by the blow. He struck me again as I came in, but I did not circle and parry; I drove for the kill. My first blow missed, my second caught him in the ribs and I saw his jaw go slack.

He was soft . . . in good enough shape for his time and place, but nothing like the ruggedness a man acquired working on the plains and the desert. There were others at the school who were better, I think, but they were awed by his size and his boxing skill.

So I smashed at him with both hands, going under his left lead and whipping both hands to his body; then, stepping back, I smashed him in the face. It broke his nose, but I followed it up with two more blows, and he fell.

The fight had lasted less than a minute, but if I had expected to win their friendship by that fight, I would have been mistaken. The talk I heard afterward accounted for that. I had not fought like a gentleman. I was too *rough*. As for me, I had learned only one way to fight—to win.

The following day I was dismissed from the school. When I was packing, Wickes came to the door. "Dury? Here's someone to see you."

There were three of them—Ashmead, Travers, and Allen. All of them were boys I knew only by sight.

Ashmead, a tall, blond, handsome boy, walked up to me and thrust out his hand. "Look, Dury, I am sorry to see you go. I think it dashed unfair of them."

"It is all right," I said. "I have been wanting to go home."

His eyes were bright with excitement. "Where is it you live? In Texas?"

So I stopped packing and sat down and told them about it. I told them about the country in all its wild beauty, about the killing of my parents, and my long captivity by the Apaches. I told them how the Apache made his bow and where he found his food, and about the Sierra Madre and my escape from there, riding alone across two hundred miles of wild country, in any mile of which I might have been shot by the Apaches for escaping, or by the Mexicans as an Apache.

"Is it true they carry pistols?" Travers asked.

So I opened up my bag and took out my own Colt army revolver, Model 1848. It was a .44 rim-fire six-shooter with an eight-inch barrel. "Be careful with that," I said as Travers reached to take it up. "It's loaded, and has a hair trigger."

He drew his hand back quickly, but they gathered around, staring at the gun as if it were a live thing. It was battered and showed its use, but it was a good weapon still.

"If they had known you had this," Ashmead said, "you'd have been out of school before this."

Suddenly I was a hero, regarded with awe. I had in my possession a genuine western-style pistol.

We talked until it was time to go to my train, and they came to the station with me, my three new friends and Larry Wickes.

There was nothing for it but to return to Sotherton Manor, and I did not want to go. I had not expected to return a failure. But nothing was said of it when I arrived.

It was not until later, when Sir Richard and I were alone in his study, that he said, "You hurt that boy. You beat him quite badly."

"Yes, sir."

"The headmaster said you attacked him savagely."

"He struck me, sir, and I whipped him."

"But did you have to do it so brutally?"

"I know of no other way to fight, sir. One fights to win. I would not know how to fight any other way. It was he who began the fight, and I had tried to avoid it—so much so they were saying I was afraid."

"Well," he said ironically, "they do not think so now." He studied me for a moment, and then asked, "What do you plan to do now?"

"Return home, sir. To Texas."

"We would like to have you stay. My wife and I, we would like it very much if you stayed."

"Thank you, sir. You've given me every opportunity, but I keep thinking of it back there. Whatever there is in life for me is back there. I—I am not cut out for this."

"This morning I was speaking to George Travers. He is an old friend of mine, you know. He told me you had a revolver."

"Yes, sir."

"Aren't you rather young to be carrying a weapon of that kind?"

"No, sir. In Texas I carried one from the time I was twelve. When one lives in Apache country one must go armed."

"May I see it?"

We went up to my room and I opened my luggage and took out my worn but well-oiled belt and holster. The walnut butt of the revolver was badly scarred and the gun showed wear, but it was clean and ready for action.

He took the gun in his hands and turned it carefully. "Now, there's no nonsense about that, is there?"

"It has a hair trigger, sir."

"Yes, I suspected as much."

He handed the gun back to me. "Is it true they shoot as well as they say? One hears much talk of the gunfighters out there."

"Would you like to see me shoot, sir?"

"I would, indeed. Shall we go outside?"

He watched as I dug into my luggage for ammunition, and then we went outside. Felicia saw us and followed along. At the back of the house I asked for bottles and received several from the cook. One of these I suspended by a string from the branch of a tree. We walked back twenty paces and, turning suddenly, I drew and fired, smashing the bottle.

Without waiting for any comment, I tossed another bottle into the air, drew, fired from the hip, and smashed the bottle, and then smashed the largest fragment as it fell.

"May I try?" Sir Richard asked.

He placed a bottle thirty paces off, took careful aim, and broke it.

He glanced at the pistol. "It does have a very light pull, doesn't it?"

Suddenly he smiled. "You are an excellent shot, my boy," he said. "I would never try anything like that. And had I not seen you fire from the hip, I should not have believed it could be done with accuracy."

We walked back to the house, and for the first time since I had known her, Felicia was silent. I thought she was a bit awed. At least, I preferred to think that was how she felt, for I had had little enough luck at impressing her, and I had wanted to, very much.

Alone in Sir Richard's study, we talked for a while and then he glanced at me suddenly. "You spoke of my son's killers being punished. What was their sentence?"

"There was no sentence, sir, because there was no judge, no jury. There is no law in that region, sir, and very little in the region to which they fled."

"Then what happened?"

For an instant, I hesitated, wanting to avoid telling

him, but I could not lie to this man. "I killed them, sir."

"*You* killed them?"

"Yes, sir. Jim Sotherton was my friend—the only friend I had, in fact—and they used him rather badly."

"I see." After a minute he said, "We will say nothing of this to anyone else—they would be shocked."

"And you, sir?"

He smiled at me. "Conn, I followed a Pathan tribesman for three weeks once, before I got a shot at him. He had killed a brother officer of mine."

He filled his pipe. "It is rather a different life on the frontier, isn't it, boy?"

Sir Richard had given me one more thing before I returned to my own country. He had given me an unforgettable year of travel on the Continent.

"My sister," he told me, "willed her money to James, and James left it to go to Felicia, but to be used as I saw fit, as a protection for us in the event we came upon hard times. So I want you to take money enough from that estate to see Europe."

He denied my protests, and said quietly, "You owe it to yourself, boy. Someday you may have a family of your own, and you will want to contribute to their education. Also, you owe it to James. He would have wished it so."

My protests were not very strong in the beginning, and that quieted them forever, so I accepted money and a drawing account, and spent the next year in traveling—without ever forgetting the West.

The only thing I did not like about it, Sir Richard insisted I leave my gun with him until I returned to England.

By the time I returned to the States I was nineteen years old; the year was 1858.

That year, for a short while I was not sure whether I wished to remain in the West, but that uncertainty lasted about as long as it took me to get a saddle on a horse, mount up, and feel the wind on my face and see the long grass bending under it.

CHAPTER 6

Now, riding back to the camp on the knoll, I tried to recall a Frank Shalett from those years before my trip to Europe, but I could not remember the name. So he must be someone I had known later, or the relative of someone I'd known.

In the camp there was much speculation on who McDonald and Shalett would have coming on the train.

"He'll round up some of those Bald Knobbers," Harvey Nugent suggested. "There's aplenty of boys back in the Missouri hills who'd fight for wages."

Kate Lundy was waiting for me by her ambulance, face to the wind, a few strands of hair blowing. No getting around it, she was a handsome woman. Even among beautiful women in England or on the Continent she would have been considered so.

"What will they do, Conn?" she asked.

"It isn't what they will do. It is what *we* must do. We've got to stop that train before it gets here. We've got to turn it around and send those boys right back to where they came from."

"They'll fight."

"Sure—if we give them the chance."

That outfit we had, they were ready for it, I could see that, and man for man I'd match them with any bunch of fighting men anywhere. Only we were spread out too much. Priest and Naylor were over at the new town. Red Mike was off down the trail somewhere, rounding up more fighting men. Our fence ran down both sides of the town, so my force was split in two by the enemy. And that wasn't good at all, for the fence must be guarded or they'd get out there and cut our wire.

So far, we had turned away several herds, and I could imagine what they were thinking down there in town. Some of them would quit and go, especially the ones who had never favored McDonald or his ways, but there was no quit in Aaron McDonald himself.

"I'm going to head them off, Kate," I said. "I'm going to take a few of the boys and head them off before they are ready for us."

D'Artaguette I wanted. That Frenchman would stand hitched, come hell or high water. Red Mike wasn't here, but I'd take Meharry, Rowdy Lynch, Gallardo, and Battery Mason. That should do it.

Yet the whole setup worried me because we were spread so thin, and those men down there in town were not fools. Most of them were fighting men, and many of them had bought lots or built houses and so had at stake something more than merely a desire to fight.

"Kate," I said, "we're going to get some wire cut, and we're going to have to stand for it."

Her face hardened, for Kate Lundy was a fighter, too, and there was no more give in her than there was in McDonald.

"While I'm gone they might mount a real attack," I went on, "and we're outnumbered, so I want you to pull the men off the wire. On this side of town, bunch them here, well dug in and ready to make a stand.

"Over on the other side they can pull back to that

pointed hill where the rocks are. By day the wire can
be pretty well covered from those two places, so let
them hole up and keep to those places until I get
back."

The trouble was, of course, that we did not know
what McDonald was thinking, and I knew better than
to lowrate the man.

By day Kate Lundy missed nothing. She left the
direction of the struggle in my hands, but her sug-
gestions when she made them were good and to the
point. For as long as I had known her, I had never
seen her quite like this, and much as I had respected
her before, I felt even greater admiration now.

Bedded down as I was, night after night, not far
from the ambulance where she slept, I knew that she
lay awake, her light burning into the small hours, and
sometimes I heard those low sobs as she wept alone.

For she was truly alone now—her husband killed
so long ago, and now Tom gone.

These had been her family, these had been her
all, and around them she had built her world. If she
managed to make her ranch from nothing into a great
success, it was more for Tom than for herself . . . and
now Tom was gone.

Within me there grew a tiny fear, but it was one
that grew as the days went on: what would she do,
what would become of her when this battle was over?

She had always been strong. Her slender body,
shaped as beautifully as a man could imagine, was
nonetheless like whipcord and whalebone. During
those first years there had been only two of us, although Tom made a riding hand very quickly. Together we rebuilt the burned cabin, we built parapets
of defense and cleared a field of fire around us. We
cleaned out the spring, dug a stone-lined trench to

bring the run off nearer the cabin, and built a stone corral.

There were both wild horses and wild cattle in the country around, and we worked from early morning until late at night rounding them up, roping and branding. We held one small herd in a grassy valley close by, trying to select from all we found the best breeding stock.

At night she gave Tom his schooling, to which, in a small way, I contributed.

Now, sitting off to one side of the fire, we talked over the tactics of the coming days. We would ride to the small station and water tank where Delgado had sent off his messages, and attempt to intercept the train there, or just beyond. We would be gone three or four days and, because we were undoubtedly spied on, the people of the town would know we were gone and would choose their time to attack.

Harvey Nugent shrugged. "Don't worry, we'll handle it."

I cannot say that I particularly liked Nugent, but he was a fighting man, and one I preferred having on my side. Every one of them had sand . . . they would stay the fight through.

Only during a lull in the talk, while we ate, I kept wishing I'd see Red Mike show up over the hill with the rest of the men we had sent for. We were going to need them.

It was an hour shy of daylight when I drew up outside the ambulance to say good-bye to Kate. She was standing beside her wagon, and she held up her hand to me.

"Conn . . . Conn . . . I can never tell you how much I owe you. I could never begin to tell you how much it has meant to me to have you with me."

We'd known each other a long time, and only once

before had she said anything like that. For a moment I could not answer her.

"I'll do my best, Kate," I said then, and added, "Be careful, Kate. McDonald would kill a woman as soon as a man. Like John Blake said, he's a witch-burner, and there's no sentiment in him."

"All right, Conn."

Nugent was there, standing by, tough, battle-scarred, a man who lived to fight. I knew that, once he'd accepted a job, he rode for the brand. There was no sell-out in him.

"Don't you worry none, Dury," he said now, "we'll hold up our end."

"You always have, Harvey," I said, and there was a flicker in his eyes at the praise.

"You know," I said in a low voice, "I'd not want to leave here if I didn't know you were here."

He threw me a look of astonishment, and then he spat, and said roughly, "You boys ride along. We're all right."

We took two head of horses per man, so we could ride harder and faster, and we went off up a draw that led away from the camp. Then we held to low ground so as not to sky-line ourselves against the horizon stars. When we were a couple of miles off we came out of the low ground and headed off across country, toward the east.

We went quietly, to leave no dust to mark our passing, for they might have scouts in the country around, and even if dust cannot be seen, the smell of it hangs in the air. We rode off to our own small destiny, six battle-hardened men, to meet an enemy whose numbers we could not know except that they were sure to be greater than our own.

How many times had western men, men such as we, ridden off to their forgotten, unwritten battles? There was a flat stone I had seen once, a stone on which was scratched the small story of five men who dared the western mountains in search of gold, five who went where no one had dreamed of going before, and when the final message was scratched, three were already dead and two were dying.

The names were scratched there, but who ever heard of any of them? Had they relatives, friends? Who waited for their return? Did anyone ever know what happened? And how many other such stories were there, stories never found on stones, of men who had no time to write messages?

These men who rode beside me were such men as had fought the ancient wars, such men as had followed their loyalties to bloody death or bloody victory since time began. If this was my time to die, then I could go in no better company.

The rolling hills and the prairie lands over which we rode were wide, and we rode the night away, until the red dawn came in the sky. At noon, when the sun was high above us, we drew up in a tiny hollow among the hills, and while one man watched for the Indians that might come upon us, we switched our saddles and remounted again.

The place toward which we rode was a lone stop on the railroad where there was a station, a telegrapher, and a saloon, a few cars standing on a side track—and nothing more.

This was the place where I hoped to learn something from the telegrapher about the train that would bring the fighting men for McDonald and Shalett.

By mid-morning we were coming up to the station. We had stopped, scouting the place from a distance and out of sight. Nobody seemed to be around, but I was worried.

McDonald was no fool, and by now he must know

we were gone, and he would attack before the day was out, or would make some move. He had the men. He had the fire power.

He might do more than that, he might attempt to cut us off, to destroy us. He must have guessed where we were going, although I doubted that he knew why. He was not the sort of man to expect six men to attempt to stop fifty or more.

Rowdy Lynch cut away from us and started a wide ride around the station. Gallardo started in the opposite direction to head off anyone who might try to circle away from Rowdy.

The rest of us waited to give them a start, and then rode down to the station.

The telegrapher, I saw, was a slim, wiry young Irishman whose face looked like a map of the island itself. He was in his early twenties, and had a tough, hard-bitten, devil-may-care air about him that I liked.

"Meharry," I said, "it looks like a job for you."

Meharry got down and strolled into the station, and we rode to the stable back of the saloon, where we left our horses.

The place was built like a fort. The stable itself was half a dugout, half a sod house, but it was strongly made. The second story of the saloon overhung the lower like a blockhouse, so nobody could attack doors or windows without being exposed from above. There were portholes in the second-story floor so that a gun might be fired directly down at anyone attacking the doors below. From a spike near one of those portholes, a withered, dried-up Indian's hand hung by a wire, and I recalled hearing the story of that hand on my last trip up the trail.

The saloon had been attacked, and one Indian, thinking there might be a door, had thrust his hand through the porthole, grasping for a hand-hold. It had been promptly lopped off, and then hung there as a reminder to others. Nobody had ever attempted that again.

The big room of the saloon was empty except for the saloonkeeper himself, who was bartender as well. He was leaning on the bar reading a month-old newspaper.

"Third time I've read that," he said, "but there ain't anything else to read. I've memorized all the labels on the cans, and on every bottle in the house."

"I've a book in one of my saddlebags," I said. "I'll leave it with you."

"Ain't one of them pony express novels, is it? I sure like to read them. Makes it seem mighty exciting out here."

He placed a couple of bottles on the bar. "Fact is, it was reading them books started me out here. So far I've had no chance to save ary a white woman from the redskins. Come to consider it, I ain't seen but one white woman, and no Indian would have her."

"It's a history," I said regretfully.

"Hey, now that's fine!" He was genuinely pleased. "By the time I figure out what they're gettin' at, and how it really must have been, this here will be a set-tled-up country with kids walking to school."

"Do you think that will ever be?" D'Artaguette said.
"Why not?"

"How's business?" I asked.

"You makin' jokes? Ain't been a dozen people in here this month. There just ain't no business, none a-tall. But it'll pick up . . . time the cattle start movin'."

"I haven't seen a soul in the country around," I commented, casually. "Who comes to a place like this?"

The bartender touched a finger to his mustache. "Mostly folks to use the wires . . . right now my guess would be there's a war startin' west of here. You boys want to use those guns, you head west.

"Man in here t'other day, askin' about fightin' men. Flanagan, down to the station, he told me he wired for riflemen."

D'Artaguette shook his head in a puzzled way. "Me, I'm just a cowman," he said, "headin' south to meet a herd that's overdue, but I wouldn't know where to get a lot of fighters if I wanted them. Maybe back in Texas."

"Hell, you don't need to go that far! Missouri, Arkansas . . . eastern Kansas . . . there's plenty of men who don't care who they shoot. You take Missouri, now. Those squirrel shooters over there, they'd shoot anybody, you pay them enough.

"Take that James outfit, now. James and them Youngers—they've got a lot of men around them, men who run with them now and again. You could hire that lot. Times are bad, dry year, and that bunch don't take much to honest farmin'. That Jesse, now. Don't know as he ever earned an honest dollar. Took to horse-thievin' even before he joined up with Quantrell."

D'Artaguette traced circles with his glass on the bar, and I kept silent. If we just listened, this man was going to tell us all we needed to know.

Suddenly, a thought occurred to me. "Get you that book," I said, and walked outside.

Meharry was standing outside the station talking to Flanagan. Going out to the horses, I took the battered copy of Carlyle's *French Revolution* from my saddlebag. Books were hard to come by, and I'd brought this one from England, but I'd read it twice and it might be a cheap price to pay for a friend in the right place.

While I was out there I took a careful look at the

hills around. They seemed innocent of trouble, but I trusted them not at all.

Battery Mason was standing at the corner of the building. "Keep an eye out," I said. "I've a hunch."

Where the station stood, the ground was flat, but it swelled slowly up into low hills not over a quarter of a mile away. Such country is deceptive, and although it seemed open, and surprise an impossibility, one could take it too much for granted, and surprise was possible. I had seen it happen in just such terrain.

When I went back inside the saloon the bartender was setting them up. He grinned broadly at the sight of the book. "Well, now! There's a good piece of book for you! Thank you, mister! Thank you kindly."

He turned it admiringly in his hands, then hefted it. "Now, that there," he said speculatively, "why, that should keep a man in readin' for a year, or nigh to it."

"It's a fine book," I said.

He turned the pages. "Yep! Like I thought! Mighty full of big words, and some I never seen before! Now, I like that. I admire a writer who has words . . . time I figure out what he means by them, a book will last me twice as long. Thank you again, sir!"

Battery Mason stepped to the door. "Conn," he said, "somebody's comin'!"

CHAPTER 7

It has been given me that I live in the moment, with an awareness heightened by every impression of the senses. No doubt a part of it was natural to me, but it was also conditioned in me by Jim Sotherton.

He lived in such a way, and he was forever commenting to me on how few people actually lived *now*. Most people, he said, exist in an emptiness between memory anticipation, but never live *in the moment*.

Whatever natural tendency I may have had toward living in the moment was developed and increased by Sotherton's comments, and by his own awareness.

Now when I stepped from the door of the saloon into the bright sunlight, I stood for a moment to let my eyes become accustomed to the change of light. As I stood there on the weathered boardwalk, I looked down at the gray boards, at the cracks, the slivers, the places where some idle hand had whittled with a knife, and I was aware of the warm sun and the silence, of water dripping from the water tank used by the railroad into a trough used by passing riders. And then I looked up and walked to the end of the porch with Mason.

The air was startlingly clear. Far away in the sky was a puff of cloud against the blue. The smooth flow of the rolling hill was a soft green with the new grass

growing, and I stood there, feeling the weight of the
gun against my leg, the sun on my shoulders, squint-
ing my eyes against the distance, watching the rider
on the far-off hill.

He was one man alone, and he rode a mule. That
was obvious from the gait of the animal. Sunlight
gleamed on a rifle barrel.

Battery Mason swore suddenly, then he said, "Conn,
you know more than one man who rides a mule?"

"Not in this country."

It was Hoback. He was coming on along the flank
of the hill, taking his time.

A little chill went through me, the sort of chill you
have when they say somebody has stepped on your
grave.

The air was completely still, and I could smell the
dust in the space—scarcely to be called a street—
between the saloon and the station. Around the tight
little knot of buildings all was bare, open to the sky
and the wind. Only the distant rider moved.

Lowering my eyes for a moment, I saw an ant strug-
gling with some tiny object, but an object larger than
itself. Battery was leaning against the corner of the
saloon, and I knew what was going through his mind.
. . . That was Bill Hoback, the Dutchman, out there.

We had not sent for him, and the chances were he
was not riding in search of a job, so he must have
been hired by McDonald or by Frank Shalett. Mc-
Donald was unlikely to have heard of the Dutchman,
so it must have been Shalett's idea.

Shalett again. Now, who was Shalett?

Nobody needed to tell me, or Battery Mason, who
the Dutchman was. He was a man-hunter. A man who
stalked other men to kill—to kill for cash. He hunted
men the way other men hunted buffalo, or deer. He
stalked them, killed them, collected his price.

For a man riding a mule who was so well known by chuck-wagon yarns, the Dutchman managed to drop out of sight whenever he wanted. But he was known as a fast and deadly accurate shot with any kind of weapon. Handy with a pistol, though he relied more on a rifle or shotgun, both of which he habitually carried.

Nobody knew how many men he had killed; probably he didn't know himself. Does a butcher keep track of the beeves he slaughters?

By now he had seen us, of that I was sure, but he was coming on, riding right down to the station.

Suddenly, I felt a twinge of worry. Where was Rowdy? Where was Gallardo?

Battery was thinking the same thing. "Ain't heard a shot," he commented, "but those boys should ought to be back."

From where we stood we could hear the low murmur of voices from the station platform where Meharry stood with Flanagan. They had seen the rider, too, and were watching him, for in all that vast landscape he was the only moving thing.

"Makes a man think, seein' him around," Mason commented. "I'd sooner be in a dark room with a cougar."

"Do you know him?"

"Don't want to. But I was out in Colorado when he was around there."

Meharry stepped down off the platform at the station and walked slowly across the street. As he came up on the boardwalk he said, "You ever hear about his contracts?" he asked. "Anybody found dead with a bullet in them . . . anybody of those he's supposed to get . . . and he gets paid."

My eyes returned to the rider. Never had I deliberately started out to kill a man who had done no harm to me or mine. I had killed two of the men who had murdered Sotherton, but that was my job, for he had been my friend and my employer, and in that country you fought for the brand you worked for.

This was different. This time I was going to have to order a man killed, or kill him myself, and of the two I preferred the latter.

This man must die, and he must die at once, for we might never see him again . . . but he would be sure to see us. And one by one we would die. The man was more deadly than any Comanche.

Did he know we were here? I thought not. He had come unexpectedly into a trap.

He was close enough now for us to see him clearly, and he was older than I had thought. He might have been fifty, or perhaps older. He was a short man with a lean, sharp face and the coldest eyes I had ever seen.

He came riding up to the saloon and dismounted, tying his horse to the hitch rail. He merely glanced at us, then went inside.

Meharry moved over beside me. "Conn, I had a talk with Flanagan," he said. "He's going to talk over the wire with a despatcher back up the line. Maybe he can learn something."

When I went back inside, Hoback was standing at the bar, and he carried his shotgun slung from his shoulder, the butt up and about level with the top of the shoulder, the barrel dangling near his right hand. It was the first time I'd seen a gun carried that way.

He was half turned, so that his back was not to the door, and I went up to the bar and stood close to him, so close he could not get the shotgun into action if he wanted to.

There was no sense in beating around the bush with

a man like this, and I had always believed in direct methods.

"You just rode in, Hoback," I said. "Did you see a man of mine out there in the hills?"

His eyes flickered the merest bit when I called him by name, but he said, "I saw nobody."

"I hope you didn't," I said.

He let that ride for a minute or two, but it worried him, and finally he said, "Why?"

"Because if you killed him I'm going to kill you."

Fear rode before this man wherever he went, like a ghost horseman, and he was not accustomed to such direct talk. He started to speak, but I gave him no chance.

"I know who you are, Hoback, and why you are here. I also know how you get paid. Now listen to this. If one of my men, any one of them, is killed by any means whatever, I shall hunt you down and kill you like you've killed others."

Down the bar Battery Mason was holding his breath, and the bartender had moved as far away as he could get, but Bill Hoback had been taken off balance and was speechless. I did not give him a chance to reply or to get set. My left side was almost against him, and he had no chance to lift the shotgun, or even to lift his right hand without brushing me. His left hand rested on the bar.

"You get paid no matter who kills the man you're after, so we'll use the same rule you like. If any one of my men is killed, in any way whatsoever, we kill you."

He was sweating, but I'd never seen a man's eyes so mean, so bitter with a fury he could not let out.

"You're Conn Dury," he said.

"That's right, Dutchman. I'm Conn Dury; and if you'll recall, I spent part of my years living with the

Apaches. I could follow your sign across a flat rock . . . I could follow it by the smell."

He pulled back, trying for distance, but I moved right with him.

"You got no call to jump me," he protested. "I done nothing."

"And you aren't going to." As I spoke, a plan came to me suddenly. "In about half an hour there's an east-bound train due in here. We're putting you aboard."

"Like hell!" he said. "I'll—"

My back hand took him across the mouth, and he staggered. His right hand dropped to his shotgun and it swept up, faster than a man could draw a gun, his right hand going back to the action, the left catching the barrel—a movement so incredibly swift that I'd never have believed it possible.

Yet I had followed him up, and as his gun came up I slapped the barrel aside. Had I been two feet further away, he would have blown me apart. As it was, the shotgun went off harmlessly with a thunderous roar in the close confines of the room, and then I hit him.

My right fist caught him on the jaw and knocked him sprawling. Leaping after him, I kicked the gun from his hands. He lay there, staring up at me, blood trickling from a split lip from my backhand blow.

A gun butt was visible in his waistband and his hand hovered close to it. I stood waiting, my own gun in its holster.

"Go ahead," I said. "Just go ahead and try it."

He was no gunfighter in the sense that I was, that some of the others I had with me were. It might have been that he was faster and more accurate than any of us, but it simply was not his way of fighting. There was an instant when I thought his rage might bring him to draw, but the instant passed, and slowly his muscles relaxed. This man was not going to risk dying, He was a killer from ambush, a sure-thing killer.

"Meharry," I said, "tell Flanagan there will be a passenger on the next train—a passenger who will ride in a cattle car."

He lay there, resting on one elbow, hating me.

"Take his gun, Mason. Then go out and look over his outfit. We're going to pay him for it and let him ride out of here without it."

"He'll buy another."

"No," I said, "he's going out of here broke. We'll send the money, and whatever he has in his pockets, to the post office in Joplin. He can pick it up there."

But when we stood on the platform watching the caboose of the train disappearing down the track toward the east, I had no idea that this was the end of the Dutchman. He would be back. I had only postponed the inevitable.

"You should have killed him," D'Artaguette commented thoughtfully. "You should have taken the slightest move he made as excuse and killed him, once you had him on the floor. Nobody would have blamed you."

"That's my trouble," I replied. "I've killed men, but I am not a killer."

We went back inside, and as the afternoon had waned into dusk, we ordered supper and sat down to wait for it. Several times one of us went outside, and at last I saw Rowdy Lynch and Gallardo coming down the slope together. I hadn't been that relieved in a long time.

The sky turned blood-red, and the red bathed the hills in soft crimson or pink; the night closed around us and gathered the hills into shadow, and the stars lit up their lamps.

"Conn," Rowdy said, "we're late because we found some tracks out there."

Gallardo had been the first to cut a trail, and it was the trail of a single rider—not the Dutchman—and Gallardo had followed it, for it led where he had been directed to ride.

Rowdy Lynch, coming up from around the station, riding south, but east of the town, had come on the trail of a large herd of cattle. Following that trail, he had come on Gallardo, working out the puzzle of the tracks.

The lone horseman had met the point of the herd. Ordinarily he would never have found those tracks, because the following herd would have wiped them out; but after the meeting, the herd had been stopped, and turned back again to the south.

"*South?*" I exclaimed.

"That was the way of it, Conn. And to me it spells trouble."

That lone rider might have been somebody from the herd itself, somebody who had gone ahead to look out for a good holding ground, and for water. I suggested as much.

"No, that rider was George Darrough, that buffalo-hunter friend of McDonald's. I'd know that horse of his anywhere. He rides an appaloosa he swapped from some Indian some time or other, and that horse has the smallest, prettiest feet I ever did see. I've seen those tracks before. That rider was George Darrough."

"What do you think, Rowdy?"

"Why, I've been studying on it, all the way in here. Me and Gallardo figure we've put a loop on the idea. Darrough came out to pick up a herd."

"To ship from the town?"

"Maybe." He paused. "Conn, you ever seen what a stampeding herd can do to a wire fence?"

He was right, of course. A stampede of cattle could sweep such a fence out of existence. It could also trample anybody guarding that fence . . . trample them, churn them into mud.

"We've got to go back, Conn." D'Artaguette's face was pale. "God almighty, they'll run the herd right over the boys!"

"Not if they are where they should be," I said, "and not if they shoot down some steers for a barricade."

But Kate . . .

I was scared to death. If we rode, starting now, we could make it. The tracks were only a few hours old, and it would take time to move a herd, even a herd that maybe was being hurried along.

"Here comes Flanagan," somebody said, and looking around, I saw the red-haired telegrapher coming across the street.

He grinned, and shook a yellow sheet at us. "If you boys are hunting a scrap," he said, "you've bought yourself a mean stack of chips! There are fifty men and horses on that train. It's due in here at daybreak tomorrow . . . due to unload here."

Fifty men!

"That sort of story goes all down the line," Flanagan said. "Everybody knows something is up. Any time fifty men and fifty horses with a wagon for supplies and ammunition is put aboard a train, we know there's going to be hell to pay."

"Who are they?"

"Ozark Mountain boys. Hillbillies from Missouri and Arkansas."

Fifty men . . . fifty riflemen—dead shots, or they'd not have been chosen. They would pick us off like squirrels.

"Conn," D'Artaguette said, "what about that herd?"

For a long moment I stood there, hesitating, and

then I said, "We'll have to trust it to Kate and the boys. We came out here to do a job, and we're going to do it."

"To fifty men?" D'Artaguette protested.

"That's only eight apiece," Rowdy said, "with two spares. Conn, you leave me one of them spares, will you?"

The saloon door opened. "You boys goin' to eat?" a voice called. "I got it on the table!"

It was full dark now, a soft prairie night, and the stars were out.

Soon the coyotes would be calling.

CHAPTER 8

Flanagan joined us at the table, glad to have company. His was a lonely job, and it needed a man of a very special kind of courage. He sat at his telegraph key in the small station with a pistol only inches from his hand, a shotgun and a Sharps .50 buffalo gun close by.

Twice he had been completely isolated—once when Indians had torn down his wires to make copper ornaments of them, and again when buffalo, that used the posts to scratch themselves, pushed over several of them.

We had all kinds in the West. D'Artaguette and Meharry were college men; the former had been educated in Paris and Quebec, the latter in Dublin and London. All the education Rowdy Lynch ever got he picked up in the middle of a horse's back. I'd never even seen him read a newspaper. As for Battery Mason, he had been a tough kid in the slums of New York and had drifted west because that's where people were drifting, and he stayed on to become more western than the native-born westerner.

Gallardo was a special case. His family had come to New Mexico with the first settlers. They had schools and churches there before Captain John Smith landed in Virginia, and they had grown children before the

Pilgrims landed at Plymouth Rock. Gallardo had attended a church school in Santa Fe for several years, when not punching cows on his father's ranch.

I looked around the table, and was glad it was these men I had with me.

"Flanagan," I said, "you know your railroad. I need a place back up the line where there's a grade steep enough to slow a train down, a place where we could board the train without stopping it."

"Sorry, but there's nothing like that within the distance you could ride in the time you have. Nothing I can recall, at least."

"Why not here?" Meharry suggested. "When they start to leave the train."

At such a time, there was confusion and it might be done, but there was risk. Undoubtedly some would be half asleep, but a few would be awake enough to resist; and once it started, the others would be quickly alerted. We could hurt them, but we could not win; and nobody needed to tell me how difficult it is to get out of a fight once one is involved . . . that would be hardest of all.

I felt no certainty about what was best to do. Nobody felt like talking, and when supper was over, I walked outside.

It was very still. A few crickets talked from the grass at the side of the building. Near the station, a pile of ties was stacked, and strolling over, I hoisted myself up and sat down on them. Only a little time remained, and I hadn't an idea of what I was going to do.

If the men we had ridden here to stop managed to get past us and reach the town, then we must withdraw, our fight at an end. Even at this moment, back there at the town, our friends might be fighting a last-ditch struggle against the townsmen, for the latter would surely try to cut the fences while we were absent.

Those men back there with Kate, like these with me, were men who rode for the brand. When they accepted a man's pay they not only worked for him, they fought his battles. It was as simple as that. Life offered them no other loyalties than their country, the man they worked for, and the men they worked beside. When they went into the fight they would go trusting me, and I hadn't a plan.

Getting up, I prowled restlessly among the buildings. We might be able to take the men by surprise, for they would not be expecting us here. But there would be others riding on the train, I wanted no reckless shooting.

Somewhere out in the darkness, miles away but drawing nearer every moment, was the train bearing fifty armed fighting men. Somehow or other, I had to come up with a plan.

Yet at this moment I could not marshal my thoughts, and they went back to that Texas morning, with Kate standing beside the fire in the bleak dawn, the smell of charred timber in the air, mingling with the smoke of the fresh fire and the smell of coffee. That was the morning when she had told me she was not leaving—that they had come to settle, and settle they would.

What arguments had I to offer to such a woman? Yet I tried.

"Mrs. Lundy," I said, "you'd better give it some thought. Right over there, only a little way off, is the Comanche Trail—the route they follow on their raids into Mexico. And this is Apache country too. Believe me, this is no place for a lone man, let alone a woman and a youngster."

"We're going to stay," Kate said. "This is our home."

Home? It was a rock-ribbed valley in a country borrowed from the leavings of hell.

There was water, and there was grass, and there were some cottonwoods to rustle their leaves for her, but there surely was nothing else, and it was a hundred or more miles to the nearest white man . . . and God only knew where there was another woman.

The burned-out house could be fixed up to live in for the time being, and there was a piece of stone corral her husband had started to build. That was all.

"That's a fine-looking boy," I said, deciding to outflank her on the arguments. "He will need an education."

"I had a very good education," she replied, "and I can teach him myself."

"There will be no pretty clothes down here, no balls or parties, or talking with other women."

"I shall miss them."

"If it is money you need," I began carefully, "I—"

"No," she said firmly, "it is not money. I have a little—it is not that. We adopted a course of action, Mr. Dury, and my husband chose this place. It is wild, but there are cattle for the taking, and for a time at least there will be nobody to argue ownership. And by the time we are ready for it, the country will have built up to us."

"If you'll pardon me, ma'am," I said gently, "you are either a very wise and very brave woman, or a bit of a damned fool."

She smiled for the first time, and it was a lovely smile. "I wish I knew which it is, Mr. Dury. I really do."

It was true there were wild cattle if you could get the twine on them, but how she figured to do that I had no idea. Roping, tying, and branding wild cattle is a job for a man with hair on his chest. I said as much.

She looked at me in that cool way she had, and she said, "How's your chest, Mr. Dury?"

I did not answer that, but I said, "You'll have to have a house, and that one isn't in the right place."

"I know," she replied quietly; "but my husband knew little of such things, and he was trying very hard. I thought it better to help than to criticize."

The hell of it was, I found myself admiring her nerve, and I was a bit puzzled by her, too. What kind of a background had built such a woman as this? Woman? She was scarcely more than a girl.

"I was just riding through," I said, "going no place in particular. I'll help until you can find some hands."

She seemed amused. "Will you stay that long, Mr. Dury?"

She knew as well as I did that it would be a hell of a long time before she could hire anybody down here. It could be months, maybe a year, before anybody even passed this way.

"Tom," she said, turning to her brother, "get some more wood. I am going to make some fresh coffee for Mr. Dury."

While she was making it I scouted around, and before very long my respect for her husband began to grow. One of them, and it might have been him, had picked out a spot that would have been hard to beat in many ways. Admitted, the house was in a position that could not be defended, but there was water, grass, fuel, and from a nearby knoll, good observation and an excellent field of fire.

It was a small butte, actually, about an acre in extent, and a part of that was taken up by a huge pile of boulders. In among those boulders I found a spring with a nice flow of water. Bending down to drink, I felt a cool, pleasant breeze against my face, a really good draft of air coming through a hole among the rocks. The air was drawn through the hole and past the falling water of the spring.

I climbed on top of the boulders and looked around. Several of them were almost flat. In two places the surface of the butte below me was deeply cracked, one of the cracks leading out toward where Kate Lundy bent over her fire.

I knew then where I was going to build the house. But it was going to be brutally hard work.

Maybe this was just what I needed, for I'd been on the run when I crossed the Rio Grande. I was coming up out of Mexico with a killing behind me.

Luckily, most of the supplies the Lundys had brought into the Big Bend were still in the wagon, or stacked on the ground beneath it. There were tools, and a good bit of food, and it was not long before I added to it by killing a young heifer, and later a deer.

As time went on we saw nobody, and it was just as well, for we were working hard.

There was a meadow near the cottonwoods and a seep with a little standing water, and I built a crude fence around the meadow from dead-falls among the cottonwoods, and from brush and rocks. Then I rounded up some of the wild cattle and turned them in on the meadow. Picking the best ones I could for breeding stock, I branded everything I could dab my loop on. And every morning and evening I worked a bit, with young Tom helping, to get started on the house. I planned to include the spring in it, and to use the boulders around it.

Three good-sized rooms and a lookout tower would be built on top of the boulders themselves, and the rest of the house would be fitted into them on three sides. The fourth side was a sheer drop of about forty feet—straight, smooth rock without a hand-hold anywhere.

It took me two weeks to complete the first room, and when that was done we moved up there, with Tom and me bunking outside.

Working with a crowbar, and later with blasting powder, I cleared away every bit of cover within firing range of the house. At the same time I paced off distances to various objects within sight to get the exact range for accurate firing. Utilizing the deep cracks in the butte itself I built an undercover route that would take us to the stable and the corrals down below.

By the time we hired our first puncher, a Mexican renegade from across the border, we had a second room started on the new house, the original place was turned into a blacksmith shop, and we had a good stone and adobe corral finished. Meanwhile we were holding thirty head of selected breeding stock on the meadow.

It was the Mexican who saw the Comanches.

There were a dozen in the party and they were riding carelessly, not expecting to see anyone.

They saw the Mexican and he saw them at the same time, and they opened fire. He turned his horse and lit out for the ranch at a dead run. They killed his horse, but he sprang free and killed one of them as they charged down upon him. By that time both Kate and I were in action and we covered his retreat to the house.

That was the first of nine brushes with Indians during our first year, and we started a graveyard for warriors killed. By the end of that year there were seven graves up there, and the Indians used to come by to count them . . . we would sometimes find their tracks in the morning.

Each grave was marked with a coup stick or with the weapons of the departed.

Now and again the Mexican rode off across the Rio Grande, and then one time he did not return. We never knew what happened to him, but he had been a good man.

By the end of the second year we had four hands in the bunkhouse, and Red Mike was one of them. Kate found him on the Strawhouse Trail coming from the river, and he had three bullet holes in him, several days old.

We brought him to the house, nursed him back to health, and he stayed on. He never offered to explain the bullets, and we did not ask. It was simply not a polite question in that country, at that time.

By then there were thirteen Indians buried on the hill, and we rarely saw any Indians around. At least, we saw no Apaches.

Apache attacks ended the day I found Alvino cornered by four Comanches in Paint Gap. His horse was dead and they had Alvino without water on a sparsely covered hillside, with only three cartridges and half a dozen arrows left. They had him, and they knew it and he knew it.

Red Mike and I were riding south after crossing Tornillo Creek, with the Paint Gap Hills off on our right. We had it in mind to spend the night at a spring near the base of Pulliam Bluff when we heard the first shot. After a minute, there was another.

Alvino had made a desperate try to escape from the trap, but had failed. We caught the last of it, and I recognized that odd run he had, for I'd played and fought with Alvino in the Sierra Madre when I was a prisoner. He was the son of an Apache by a captured

Mexican girl, and he had become a top warrior among them. As a boy he had broken his leg, and it was badly set. Although he could use it, it was always shorter than the other.

"Injun fight," Mike commented. "Good riddance."

"That's Alvino," I said, "he was a friend of mine when I needed one."

So we pitched in and fought him out of his corner, and when he saw who I was and knew where I was living, it ended the Apache attacks on the Tumbling B.

Not that I expected it, for it wasn't in Indian nature; and Mexican mother or not, Alvino was an Indian all the way through. During a fight in the Apache *rancheria* where I was so long a captive, Alvino had pitched in and helped me, and now I had returned the favor. Taking him up on my horse, we rode back to the ranch and I roped a pony for him from our own small gather of wild stock.

The Comanches still gave us a whirl once in a while, so we had no chance to become less wary, but there were no more Apaches. In a sense, they still regarded me as one of their own, as a fighting man, at least; and my victories were something of which they could be proud, believing they had taught me the way of the warrior.

The War Between the States had been over only a few months when I rode into Kate Lundy's camp and became her foreman, and in the almost ten years since that time we had claimed over half a million acres of grazing land and we had a brand on thousands of cattle roaming over that country.

But in some ways I knew Kate no better than when I first came.

One day, several weeks after I had saved Alvino

from the Comanches, she asked me, "What did you tell that Apache about me? I saw him question you."

"He asked me if you were my woman."

There was a long moment of silence, and then she asked, "What did you tell him?"

"I told him you were. He wouldn't have understood anything else."

Her eyes avoided mine. "No . . . no, I suppose not."

That had been long ago, but it was all still clear in my mind. Thinking of it now, though, was not getting me any nearer to the solution of my problem, but remembering Alvino made me wonder how an Apache would have approached it.

The best thing I had been able to think of was to get on the train when they were all half asleep and get the drop on them before they suspected. That would be the easiest way, but Flanagan had said there was no such grade as we would need to board the train while it was moving. Had he lied? Or had he, perhaps, merely implied there was no such grade?

Flanagan was friendly, and no doubt sincerely so, but he worked for the railroad, and in his own way he no doubt rode for the brand—the railroad's brand in this case.

The Apache way would be to lie in wait, and shoot them down as they got down from the train. Apaches would have waited until all were off the train and spread out between the station and the saloon.

Once again I got up and walked around the area. There was plenty of cover for such an attack: the old stable, the saloon itself, the side-tracked box cars, the stacks of meadow-cut hay, the watering trough.

When I went back Gallardo, Mason, and D'Artaguette were rolled up in their blankets and asleep on the floor. Flanagan was leaving as I walked in.

"Irishman," I said, "you wouldn't be wiring back up the line now, would you? To warn those men?"

"Mister, this is your fight, not mine. You're in it, and whatever you do is your own business so long as you damage no railroad property and injure no passengers."

"Does that include those Bald Knobbers?"

"When they leave the train," he said, "they cease to be my affair. I'll take no hand one way or the other."

"If you ever decide to try punching cows," I said, "come down to the Tumbling B. We'll find a place for you."

He walked out, and I let him go. Meharry had been watching, and Rowdy Lynch came over to join us. They had nothing to say, but I knew what they wanted to know. They wanted to know what we planned to do, and I couldn't tell them. I simply hadn't the slightest idea of how to handle it.

And then suddenly I did know.

CHAPTER 9

The last stars hung in the sky when the train whistle called across the empty prairie and the low grass-covered hills. A huge old buffalo bull, half blind from the thick wool grown down over his eyes, lifted his huge head and stared stupidly off into the night, then rumbled a questioning challenge in his broad chest.

After a while, in the distance the train's headlight showed briefly against a far-off hill, and then there was the sound of rushing wheels, and again the long call of the whistle.

The train drew nearer and the big drivers slowed, brakes screeched, and the train rumbled to a halt alongside the station.

A light glowed from the fly-specked window of the telegraph-office window, but the saloon was dark, except for the lantern that hung over the door.

Men descended to the platform, stretching and looking around, men heavy from their uncomfortable sleep in the cramped seats of the coaches, peering doubtfully around in the unfamiliar dark.

Their eyes made out a hint of welcome in the letters faintly revealed by the feeble glow of the lantern—four letters plainly visible, and the suggestion of a fifth:

ALOON

"There she is, boys! Let's have a drink!"

The speaker started across the intervening space, and several more trailed after him, stumbling a little from the stiffness in their muscles from the long train ride.

The others remained for a few moments on the platform, peering about, and then they started to follow.

One man bent over, shielding his hand against the glass, trying to peer into the station window.

The first man to arrive at the saloon began to pound on the door. "Halloo, in there! Open up!"

All was silent.

Suddenly somebody spoke, his voice loud in the stillness. "I smell smoke!"

As if on signal, the nearest of the haystacks burst into flame, a tremendous sheet of flame billowing up from loosened dry hay at the bottom and along the side of the stack. As one man they turned to stare, astonished at the unexpected development.

And in that instant, from behind them, came the ominous sound of gun-hammers drawn back; and after that slight warning, I said, just loud enough for all to hear: "Unless you boys want to die right where you stand, drop your hardware and lift your hands!"

They had been staring into the flames, and had they turned back to face us, they would have been momentarily blinded, unable to find their targets in the darkness.

We had them cold turkey, and they knew it. Had they been less than what they were, some of them might have been killed, but they were fighting men and they knew enough to stand when caught fairly.

Only three of us were there, but two held shotguns,

the Colt revolving shotguns, and at the distance the execution would have been a fearful thing.

Battery Mason and D'Artaguette had moved down on the train, taking the last few who lingered on the station platform. And so, without a shot being fired, we took the men I had feared would destroy us. And we had taken them much as an Apache would—and as they had done, I recalled, on several occasions.

We gathered their weapons, loaded them into their ammunition and supply wagon, and hitched up their horses. Their saddle stock, brought along for immediate use, we simply turned loose on the prairies. The supplies we left at the saloon.

The hired fighters were herded into the thick-walled stables and were left under the guard of D'Artaguette, Gallardo, and Battery Mason.

The gunmen were to be fed from their own supplies; and after four days the three men I left behind were simply to ride off and leave them. Flanagan or the saloonkeeper could free them when they wished.

With Lynch driving the wagon, we started back for our own camp. We drove far into the night. As we had started late, the moon was already low before we drew near the town.

I pulled back alongside the wagon. "Rowdy," I said, "you swing wide and come up on the camp. If you hear any shooting, or things look bad, pull up and wait until daybreak. We'll find you."

"You go ahead," Rowdy said. "I can look out for myself." But he was worried.

With Meharry beside me, I struck out at a fast run across the plains. What worried me was that there was no sound, nor was there any sign of a fire. But when we drew near we saw the town was ablaze with lights, as many as if the evening had just begun on the day a cattle drive moved into the town's area.

"Conn!" Meharry caught my arm. "Look!"

It was a dead steer . . . and beyond it there was another, then five or six. Suddenly he swore, and backed off his horse. Before us was a tangle of barbed wire, dead cattle, ripped-out posts, and torn-up ground.

The herd must have hit that wire at full tilt, and our boys must have opened up on them to turn or stop the stampede.

Fear turned me cold. My skin crawled with it. For the first time in my life I felt real fear—the bitter, awful fear you feel when someone you love has been destroyed, lost beyond recall. For I knew that the men who had shot down Tom Lundy because he came calling on a girl would not hesitate to kill his sister.

We walked our horses slowly toward the knoll, hoping desperately for a challenge. And there was none.

Suddenly, almost before we wished to, we topped out on a rise.

Here, too, there were dead steers, a perfect mound of them. And beyond them the burned-out skeleton of what had been Kate's ambulance.

"Conn," Meharry said in a voice torn with emotion, "there's a body here."

He swung down, bending over close. "Cold," he whispered. "He's been dead a while."

Then he stood up. "It's Will Joyce, one of Pollock's men."

Dismounting, I walked on with him, and a bit further on we found Van Kimberly. Van was one of our own Tumbling B boys, one who had stayed with Tod Mulloy to cover Tom's leaving of town the day he spoke to Linda McDonald.

We found a dead horse, the remains of a campfire, some stacked-up and burned bedrolls.

The townsmen had stampeded the herd against our wire, and then over the camp. And they had followed along to kill whoever remained.

On the further slope of the hill we found another of Pollock's men, recognizable only because of the Lazy P burned into his holster. He had been trampled to death by the herd.

"She isn't here, Conn," Meharry said in a low voice. "She got away."

"Maybe."

"No use looking on the other side of town. If there was anybody over there, they'd still be fighting."

"McDonald might have pulled off at dark."

"We'd have heard shooting, Conn. This fight is hours old."

He was right, of course, and if any of our lot had been left alive they would have pulled out.

For where? For the new town, Hackamore, of course. Priest and Naylor were there, and the rest of Matt Pollock's outfit.

"Conn . . . they are loading wagons down there." Meharry was staring off toward the town. "I can tell by the way the lanterns are moving."

"Pulling out?"

Meharry hesitated, as if making up his mind. "No, Conn, I think they are going to hit the new town. There are too many rifles down there . . . every time one of those lanterns passes a man I can catch the glint of metal. If they could wipe out Hackamore, they might recover the business they've lost."

We would need every man, then, need them desperately, and three of my best men were back there guarding the imported gunmen.

I made up my mind suddenly. "Meharry, ride back

and tell Rowdy what's happened. Tell him to swing wide around the town and head for Hackamore. He'll be alone, so tell him to be damned careful. There will be Indians to think of, too."

"All right." But he hesitated. "Maybe I should stay with him. We could use those guns and ammunition at Hackamore."

"We'll need the men even more. You've got two horses. Ride like the devil."

Meharry gripped his Winchester. "Conn . . . a shot into one of those lanterns might give them plenty to do."

"No." I will admit I was reluctant to say it. "We're not fighting women and children. Besides, Kate would never stand for it."

Meharry knew how I felt about Kate, but he said, "Conn, do you think she's alive?"

For a moment I was shaken by a terrible fear, a fear that was washed out in a frightening wave of fury such as I had never felt before.

"If they've killed Kate," I said. "I'll personally hunt down every man of them and kill them where they stand."

Meharry gathered his reins. "I'll hurry, Conn," he said, and was off into the darkness, leaving me alone among the torn bodies of the unfortunate cattle, and near the fallen men who had given their lives. We would return to bury them. There was no time now if other men were not to die, for Hackamore was believing itself safe.

First, I dismounted and switched saddles. The weapons of the dead men had been taken, their pockets rifled. But all wore belts of ammunition that we might need, so I stripped off the belts and hung them around the saddle horn. I remounted and, leading my spare horse, I started off into the night.

Soon I must rest, but first I needed distance between myself and the town. I needed to feel that I was on my way.

By day I might have read the tracks and known what had happened on that hill, but now there was nothing to do but strike out toward the west, and hope the survivors of the attack had made it through.

Four miles west and south of the town I rode up to a slough, dismounted, and picketed the horses on the grass in the bottom of the hollow. Then I retreated into the edge of the tall reeds and, wrapped in my blanket to keep the mosquitoes off my face, I went to sleep.

With the first gray light I was once more in the saddle and headed west.

All around me was the vast sea of grass, the gray-green untouched miles where only buffalo and antelope grazed, unmarked except by a wandering Indian and the twin tracks of his travois. Steadily, I rode on, keeping off the sky lines, and watching my back trail with care.

Here and there I saw buffalo tracks, usually in twos and threes, heading south. At noon I switched horses, took a couple of swallows of water, and bit off a chunk of jerked beef to chew as I rode.

A faint wind blew from the south, the sky was very clear, and there was no sound except the drum of my own horses' hoofs on the ground. Once, circling around a butte, I left the horses in a hollow where they would be visible to me, and scaled the butte to look over the country.

It was a vast emptiness, that stretched in every direction—only the grass bending before the wind in long waves like the sea, only the faint sound of the wind brushing over the miles of whispering grass.

If all went well, I would reach Hackamore sometime tomorrow. McDonald and his crowd, coming from the town, would need much longer, with their wagons. But even as I thought of that, I realized they would not wait for the slow-moving wagons, which would carry only supplies to be used later, in the event the fight lasted longer than the initial attack. They would undoubtedly mount a large party of horsemen who would push right through to the attack.

Shortly before sundown I rode down into a small hollow, choked with willows and brush, where there was a trickle of water from a spring. After watering my horses, I staked them out, refilled my canteen, and switched saddles again. Tired as I was, there was no time for sleep.

With a boot in the stirrup, about to step into the saddle, I heard something stirring in the willows.

Instantly, I was on the ground, my Winchester at the ready.

There was silence.

Glancing at my two horses, I saw their ears were pricked and their nostrils flaring. I spoke to them gently and moved ahead, walking with care to make no noise. Peering through the leaves, I saw a saddle horse cropping grass not fifty feet away.

I returned for my own horses and led them forward, alert for the rider. But when we came into sight, the horse looked up quickly, then came toward us at a rapid trot, whinnying.

The horse was a sorrel from our own remuda, wearing the brand of the Tumbling B. The saddle was Kate Lundy's saddle, and there was blood on the pommel.

My mouth felt suddenly dry. Gathering up the reins, I mounted my own horse and started forward, back-tracking the horse.

The tracks led back up to the prairie, and as it seemed that I might have to ride some distance, I rigged a lead rope for Kate's horse, and started on again.

There was little daylight remaining. The sun was going down and there would be a brief twilight. And when darkness came I could go no further, but must wait until it was light enough to see tracks again in the grass.

The horse had trotted here, walked there, stopped to crop grass, then had started on again. It was a once-wild mustang that we had captured and broke to ride ourselves, and he was no stranger to wild country.

The light faded. I stood up in my stirrups and my eyes searched the ground, but I saw nothing. No one standing, no one walking, no body lying on the grass.

In the distance, along the horizon, clouds were forming . . . thunder clouds. The air was growing closer, heavier. I moved on, riding parallel to the faint trail. Glancing ahead, I saw the trail across the grass like a faint silver streamer lying along the ground and, touching a spur to my horse, I rode on at a gallop.

The clouds were piling up rapidly. One of them gleamed suddenly with far-off lightning.

If the rain came before I found her, the trail would be washed out. In all this vast sweep of prairie there would be no hope of finding Kate Lundy.

Suddenly, from the southeast, another trail appeared . . . three unshod ponies. That meant Indians.

Drawing rein, I looked around carefully. With three horses and my weapons, I offered a rare prize for any Indians, and in this country, at this time, they would probably be Kiowas, the most feared of all the tribes of the southern plains.

The Indians had paused too, studying the lone trail they had come upon. They had ridden along it, one Indian going one way, the others the other. Quickly they had made up their minds—this was a lone, riderless horse.

The rider was somewhere to the east and south, and that was the way they had gone.

Swearing wildly, I spurred my horse and rode desperately into the night, down into a hollow, up over a rise. Those Indians had found the trail within the last hour.

Thunder rumbled in the distance . . . lightning flashed. A long wind rustled the grass.

Suddenly I topped out on a rise and looked upon a strange tableau.

Kate Lundy stood alone in the midst of a wide open space, facing three Indians. She was standing very straight and facing them, and they were staring at her. Now they turned suddenly to look at me. None of them wore paint. One of them had an antelope behind his saddle.

Slowing my pace, my rifle ready in my right hand, I rode down to them.

They looked at me, then at the saddled horse. Any Indian would know at once it was the horse they had been tracking.

"How!" I said.

"How!" they replied. And then one of them pointed a rifle at Kate. "You squaw?"

"Yes," I said.

They looked at me with respect. "Brave warrior!" one of them grunted, his eyes seeming almost to twinkle a little. "Heap brave!"

Then, wheeling their horses, they rode off over the plains, whooping and yelling.

"What did you do to them, Kate?" I asked.

Her face was very pale, and there was blood on her left sleeve and on the side of her dress, for she had been wounded in the arm. "I told them I was not alone . . . that I had run away from my husband and he was following me."

One of them, she added, had started toward her and she had produced a knife . . . her only weapon . . . and told him she would cut his heart out if he touched her.

Obviously they were a hunting party, looking for no trouble, and had been amused by her courage in facing them. Had she shown the slightest fear, the situation would have been otherwise.

Swinging down, I caught her as she staggered. Her legs stiffened under her. "Conn . . . I'm afraid I'm going to faint."

"You?" I was appalled. "I don't believe you know how!"

And at my words she laughed weakly, but she did not faint.

The clouds were piling higher. "Kate, we've got to find shelter. That's going to be one hell of a storm."

When she was in the saddle I started to tie her in place, but she pushed my hands away. "I can still ride!" she protested.

The only shelter I knew of was in the hollow from which I had lately come. There was a sort of cave there under the thick branches of a gnarled old tree, half torn from the earth in some long-ago storm. Willows grew close around, and there was shelter there for both of us and for the horses.

Leading off at a gallop, I started back over the trail. The storm was drawing near, the wind blowing so that it was difficult to catch one's breath. It was almost dark now, but I held my direction across the wind, watching in every flare of lightning for a glimpse of the trees.

We saw the rain coming before it reached us. Black clouds covered the upper sky, but moving along the horizon was a lighter band of rain. When it reached us I knew we would be drenched. Suddenly, in a white flare of lightning I saw the wind-whipped tops of the trees.

"We're going to make it!" I yelled . . . but we did not.

The rushing wall of water caught us with only twenty yards to go, and within a few feet we were drenched to the skin. In the hollow, there was some shelter from the mighty rush of wind, and swinging down, I led the horses into the black cavity under the tree. It was quieter there, and they seemed glad to be free of the wind and most of the rain.

With my bowie knife I hacked branches from the willows and worked them into the branches above us to make a thicker roof for our little shelter. The bodies of the horses, between us and the opening, helped some, and the thickness of the branches above, the inclined trunk of the tree, and the brush around us gave added protection.

There had been no time before to get my slicker, but now I got it from behind my saddle, with the two blankets I carried. Using the slicker for a screen against the wind, we each wrapped in a blanket and huddled together against the storm. And there, exhausted, we both fell asleep.

At daybreak, with the storm gone, I built a small fire and made coffee and a thick broth of jerked beef. While it was heating, I examined Kate's arm. It was in bad shape, though the wound itself was not a serious one. The bullet had gone through the fleshy part of the arm, causing her to lose blood. With proper care it would be all right.

Though I had learned about herbs from the Indians, I recognized none that I could see around me here. My medicine had been learned from the Apaches of the deserts and mountains, not from the Kiowas, Arapahoes or Cheyennes of the southern plains. The closest care her arm could get would be in Hackamore. So we wasted no time.

As we started to go, she looked over at me and said, "Conn, that's the second time you've told somebody that I was your woman."

"The third," I replied, and then led off to the west. And after a moment, she followed.

CHAPTER 10

Kate's story was simple enough. On the morning of the attack the men had scattered along the wire before daylight, checking for breaks. They found several cuts, which they repaired, and had started back toward camp in the first gray of dawn.

"My horse was saddled," Kate said, "for I always had a saddle horse ready for every man in case of emergency, and one for myself. Harvey Nugent saved my life. All of a sudden we heard a thunder from the west, and we looked around. There was dust in the air over the small valley in that direction. Harvey just grabbed me by the waist and threw me into the saddle."

"*Stampede!*" he yelled. "*Ride!*"

He had given her horse a cut with his rope, and it was gone with a bound. Over her shoulder she saw a herd of maddened, fear-driven steers come boiling up over the rim from the valley.

"How about the rest of them? Did they make it?"

"I don't know. My horse simply ran away with me, and we were two miles off before I got him under control. By that time it was too late to do anything, and I had been shot."

"Who shot you?"

"There was a man with a rifle. He was standing on

the hill beyond the valley from which the herd came. He was in plain sight when I looked back and saw the steers coming. Dust was rising, but it hadn't obscured the place where he stood, and I saw him as plainly as I see you now. He lifted his rifle, held his aim, then fired."

It must have been, I thought, a good three hundred yards. But a man who could see well enough to score a hit at that distance could see well enough to know it was a woman he was shooting at.

"At that distance you couldn't have recognized him."

"Oh, I'll know him!" Kate looked at me. "Conn, that man wanted to kill me. He wanted me to go down and be trampled under those hoofs, and no one would ever guess I had been shot."

"How will you know him?"

She hesitated, an instant only. "He wore a black and white cowhide vest, like you'd get from a Holstein cowhide."

How long since either of us had seen a Holstein cow? The Holstein was dairy stock, and at the moment I doubted if there were a dozen Holsteins west of the Mississippi. Certainly I'd never seen one in Texas, although I'd not say it was impossible. And the chances of two such vests in this area were slightly beyond reason.

The sky was a vast plain of blue above the gray-green of the plain below, and wherever we looked there was only the long grass bending, rippling under the touch of the wind.

"Did you see anything else that would identify the man with the cowhide vest?" I asked as we rode along. "The one who shot you?"

"Only that he seemed to be thin . . . or that was the impression I got. At the distance, I couldn't be sure."

This woman who rode beside me was the woman I loved, and the woman I had loved . . . how long? From the moment we met, I knew. Yet in all our years together I had found no way to tell her, no opportunity to talk of love. Only too rarely had I talked to women, and words did not come easy to me. And I lacked confidence in my ability to say what I meant, what I felt. Nor did I have any idea that she would listen.

Now, as we rode, my mind was filled with thoughts of her.

How many times had I, in the course of our time together, turned to look at her profile against the light. Finely made and lovely she was, strong and courageous, and fit to mother a race of sons for such a country as the Big Bend.

She was of that country and, like myself, she knew when she reached it that she had come home at last. She loved it as if born to it—the far reaches of the Big Bend country, the Bend itself, and the land beyond. From Horsehead Crossing on the Pecos to El Paso del Norte, from Fort Davis to Ojinaga or Lajitas.

That was our country, and the very names were a special kind of music to our ears; for the names were born of the country itself, names such as Slickrock Mountain and the Mule Ear Peaks, Black Mesa, Yellow Hill, and the Blue Range. Left-Hand Shut-Up and Banta Shut-In, the Chinati Mountains, Frenchman Hills, and the beautiful loneliness of The Solitario, Wildhorse Mountain, Saltgrass Draw, and the Mariscals—she knew them all, as I did.

We had ridden the land together, scouting the stark hills, seeking out the lonely water holes, or the tanks that might become sources of water after the rains. She rode with grief, and I with a restlessness born of fear that this way of life, too, might pass.

Not since I was a young boy had I know anything like a home, nor felt there was a place where I belonged. Despite the thoughtfulness of the family of Jim Sotherton, I was a stranger there; and returning to my own country, I was a stranger again.

I thought back to the fall of 1858 when, just back from England, I bought a ticket in St. Joseph for Salt Lake, twenty-one days by the stage, which stopped every few hours to let the mules graze or water. No through stage route, with frequent stations for changing horses, had yet been organized, but I did not mind the leisurely ride, for I was slowly getting again the feel of my own country.

At Salt Lake I dismounted from the stage into a town buzzing with rumors of a gold strike at Pike's Peak, so with almost the last of my money I bought a horse and a pack mule and rode over the mountains to Cherry Creek and the diggings.

On the first night, in came a husky miner who stared hard at me and then said, "Say, now, ain't you the kid who killed Morgan Rich?"

Every head turned, for it was a time when "bad men," men reputed to be bad men to tangle with, were much talked of. They were matched in many an argument, and debates raged as to who was the fastest and the best shot. Their various merits were discussed like those of race horses, foot racers, or prize fighters. And Morgan Rich had been a known man.

"That was a long time ago," I said, and turned to leave. He caught my arm.

"Aw, come now!" he protested, "let me buy you a drink!"

"I don't drink," I replied, which was almost true.

"Think you're too good to drink with me?" he demanded belligerently. "If you think I'm afraid—"

"I am sure you are not," I said, and walked out. And

when daybreak came I was far from camp, riding away.

That should have ended it, but it did not. Only two nights later a thin, dark man with greasy eyes recognized me and commented aloud, "This here's that would-be gunfighter that McCloud ran off Cherry Creek."

"You're a liar," I told him quietly, "and if McCloud says any such thing, he's a liar."

"You can't talk that way to me!"

So there it was, and if I allowed the story to continue it would hound me wherever I went. "You're wearing a gun," I said, putting it squarely up to him.

He didn't like it. He didn't want any part of what he had. He had believed me to be a bluff, and now he had been fairly called, with death lying before him like an open hand of cards . . . all black.

He was only a loud-mouth. He did not want to fight, but now he was faced with the same alternative as I, both of us caught by a way of life neither of us wanted. Yet he must fight or be treated contemptuously, as a coward. Wildly, desperately, he grabbed for his gun.

And I killed him.

It was not in me to do so, but it was the rules of the game in the land and the time in which we lived. Before the day was over, I drifted again, this time to Santa Fe.

Later, in Austin, Texas, I joined the Rangers, and for two years I rode the border on the side of the law.

The war came suddenly, unexpectedly to me, who had avoided controversy, and was often far from sources of news. But when it came I resigned from the Rangers and rode north to join the Union cavalry. And it was to Captain Edwards—now Lieutenant-Colonel Edwards—that I went.

He was a bachelor, a tall, austere man, lonely as I had been, but a man with a deep love for those same wild lands from which I came. So we sat long and talked of England and the Continent, where he had been as a boy, and then of Texas and the border country and the Indians.

My Ranger experience, my knowledge of scouting and Indian lore, qualified me in his estimation, and he convinced others. I was given a commission, and rode with Phil Sheridan's cavalry.

Sheridan looked at me coolly at first when we met. "You're a Texan?"

"Yes, sir," I said, "and when the war is over I shall be a Texan again. I simply do not approve of secession. I am fighting, sir, to preserve the Union."

"So am I," he replied.

When the war was over I had the rank of captain, and no more future than a spent bullet.

Drifting into Mexico, I encountered an old enemy, a fugitive from Texas law, now a power in Chihuahua City, and married into a good Mexican family. We had words. He was quicker to speak than to draw a gun, although he was anxious to try. He would have done better to have talked less, or talked more pleasantly.

A tall, handsome Mexican glanced at the body, and then at me. "I never liked him," he said, "but—". He shrugged. Then he said, "If you do not have a fast horse, I could lend you one."

It was a tactful suggestion, for which I was grateful. "May I buy you a drink?" I said.

His eyes twinkled faintly. "Of course . . . some other day . . . and north of the border."

In other words, to hurry would not be amiss.

When I mounted, the North Star was gleaming in the sky, pointing the way to Texas.

Days later, my horse scarcely dry from crossing the Rio Grande, I rode into the life of Kate Lundy.

And now, riding beside me, Kate jarred me from my memories. "Conn! *Look!*"

It was a dust cloud, which meant a herd of buffalo or cattle, or a large party of horsemen, and they were following a route that would shortly cross our path.

I turned swiftly, rode down into a draw, and headed out of it at a gallop, with Kate Lundy close behind me.

We could hear the thunder of the approaching hoofs, and we slowed down and walked our horses. The riders went through the draw not fifty yards behind us . . . but out of sight.

It could only have been McDonald and his men, bound for Hackamore.

When we came up out of the draw, I resumed my original route. Kate, hanging on by sheer nerve, rode up beside me. "Where are we going? This is the wrong direction for Hackamore."

It was not in me to lie to her. "You wouldn't last to Hackamore. You'd pass out and take a fall. We're riding back to town."

"To *town?*"

"You need help. There's a doctor there, and there's a bed. I shall see that you have both."

For a moment she did not speak, and then she said, "Conn, they'll kill you back there. It's you they want now. You, and perhaps me."

"Me, anyway," I agreed; "but the worst of them will have gone west toward Hackamore, and your arm is in bad shape. If it is cared for, it will be all right. You're going to have care."

"It was only a flesh wound."

"From a greasy bullet? Carried, you've no idea, how nor where? That wound needs cleaning."

When we approached the town they did not see us coming, for I used every bit of low ground possible, and the first thing they knew, we were riding up the street.

John Blake stepped out to meet me.

"Hello, John," I said. "You didn't ride with them?"

"I am the town marshal, not a hired gun hand."

"Glad to hear it. Where's the doctor?"

He glanced quickly at Kate, and I saw his face stiffen. He turned around sharply. "This way . . . Doc's in his office."

The doctor looked up as we entered. His eyes went quickly to Kate, and he leaped for her and caught her just as she started to crumple up. But she was still conscious, still fighting.

We put her on the settee, and John Blake turned away toward the window. His face seemed carved from stone.

"How did that happen? Accident?"

"It was no accident, Mr. Blake." Kate spoke clearly. "That shot was fired with every intention of killing me, by someone who knew who I was."

"Who?"

"A man in a cowhide vest—black and white cowhide."

Blake showed that he was shocked. He said to me, "What sort of man was he? Did you see him?"

"Kate saw him. I was nowhere around. Thin, she said. He was some distance off, but if he could see well enough to score a hit, he could see who he was shooting at. And we don't have any cowhands who ride side-saddle."

Doctor MacWhite was sponging off Kate's arm. It

was dark and swollen, except around the wound itself, which was raw and red.

"John," I said, "I am going to find the man who wore that vest."

He was silent, and his expression puzzled me. There was still that shocked, almost stupefied look to him.

"You know who owns that vest," I said, "and I want to know who it is."

"No."

"I'm going to find out, John."

"Leave it alone," he urged, almost pleading. "Leave it alone, Conn. She's not badly hurt—she'll be all right."

There was a sound of boots on the boardwalk, and then the door was thrust sharply open.

Linda McDonald stepped in. Behind her were a dozen of the townsmen, with rifles. "There they are!" she said. "I told you they were here."

"All right," the leader of the men said. He was a man I remembered seeing standing near Tallcott that day outside the bank. "Come on, you. Drop those guns."

John Blake stepped between us. "What's the matter with you, Burrows? Dury brought Mrs. Lundy in—she's been shot."

"That makes no difference. He's one of them, and he'll hang. And her, too," he added defiantly.

"Not while I am marshal," John Blake replied quietly.

Linda McDonald turned on him. "Pa told me you'd join them, given half a chance. He never did like you." Her face was flushed, her eyes bright. "And he left me this!"

She was enjoying herself, that much was sure. In a sense, her father was now telling off the great John

Blake. It was, to her, another illustration of his power, and she was glorying in it.

"He left me this," she repeated—"the right to tell you that you're fired!"

"What!" John Blake exclaimed in astonishment.

"That's right, Blake," Burrows said. "He told me he'd left word with Linda. If you crossed us up, you were to be fired."

Burrows liked it, too. He was a small man despite his size, and he was enjoying the putting down of a man who had so long been held up as a power in the town.

"You're not the law, Blake. You're out of it."

Kate lifted herself on her good elbow. "Do you want a job, John? I'll offer you one."

He hesitated. "No," he said finally, "I know nothing about cows."

"Then take this," Kate said. "The first thing, when this trouble started, I sent for it. I knew if anybody could keep the peace it would be you. The trouble was, I held it off. I didn't give it to you. I didn't see you, but I didn't look for you, either, and for that I am to blame."

He took the telegram, and all eyes were on him. He read it, and then he looked up at her. "You understand this? It leaves me free. No strings."

"That's the way it should be, Marshal. That's why I used what influence I had to get the appointment for you. I want no favors, nor do I want favors for anyone else."

Burrows looked from one to the other, trying to figure it out. "He ain't no marshal," he protested. "He was fired."

Linda McDonald's eyes were bright and hard. "Of course he's a marshal, Mr. Burrows," she said. "Probably a United States deputy marshal. Isn't that right, Mrs. Lundy?"

"Yes, it is," Kate replied.

John Blake turned around slowly to face Linda McDonald. "Miss McDonald," he said very clearly, "where is your cowhide vest?"

CHAPTER 11

She turned her eyes on him, her face without expression. "I do not understand you, Mr. Blake."

"You own a cowhide vest. A black and white cowhide vest. Where is it?"

She shrugged. "At home, I suppose. Where else would it be?"

"We're going there," he said; "and I'll ask the doctor to accompany us, if he is no longer needed here. I want to see that vest."

It seemed to me that she was tossing a loop inside her mind, trying to put a rope on the reason for his request. At first I thought—just for a minute—that she might have done the shooting herself. Now I was not sure.

John Blake did think so, I was sure of that. But as he started for the door, he paused. "Now let me tell you something, Mrs. Lundy. And this goes for you too, Conn. This war is over, do you hear?"

"You'd better tell that to Aaron McDonald," I suggested. "He's already killed some of my men—men defending leased land."

"That makes no difference to me," he said. "The fighting stops . . . everything else will be settled in good time."

"Will that stop the men attacking Hackamore?"

He did not answer that, but turned away from me and went out the door after Linda. It was she who paused, and her eyes looked directly into mine; then she looked away from me and at Kate.

"You will see," she said. "My father is a better man than any of you, and a stronger one. By now he has burned your silly town, and when he comes back he will show you who is in charge!"

Kate smiled at her, and for the first time Linda seemed to lose that coldness that was so much a part of her.

"I wonder what you will do," Kate said, "when your father dies."

It was not meant to be cruel. Kate was musing, as I'd seen her do before, and was genuinely curious, but Linda's expression made me wonder if the thought had ever occurred to her before. Then she was out of the door and gone, and Kate and I were alone in the doctor's office.

"You'd better get some rest," I said. "I'll sit down outside."

"Sit here," she said. She was silent for a minute, then she went on. "Conn, I'd no business starting all this. We've lost some good men."

"If you hadn't started it, the men would have," I told her honestly. "They thought the world and all of that boy."

We did not speak for a few minutes, but sat listening to the tick of the clock on the roll-top desk. Outside in the street it was still.

"Conn, I want to go home," she said presently.

"All right."

"I want you to take me home—to our home."

It was as simple as that, after all the years we'd spent together. My throat felt tight and I got up quickly and walked to the door. Then I turned toward her. "I wanted that," I said. "I've always wanted that."

"It had to come by itself, Conn. Just all of a sudden, it seems so right."

"Sure," I said, and listened to the horses coming up the street. I heard them for several minutes before the sound really got through to me—horses coming nearer and nearer, until suddenly it reached me.

Riders were coming, a lot of riders.

And then I saw John Blake standing alone in the street, standing there in his black suit, facing up the street toward the west, and those riders coming on, closer and closer.

When a voice spoke, it was Aaron McDonald's.

"Get out of the street, John Blake. We know they're here, and we want them. They're both fit for hanging, and we'll win this fight after all."

I could see them—Aaron McDonald and thirty-odd riders, but there were riderless saddles with them, too, and bodies hung over saddles, and there were men among the thirty who were in no shape for any kind of a fight. This was a well-whipped bunch—or they had been until that minute. Now they only had one man to stand against, and he was in plain sight before them.

"You're all alone," McDonald persisted, "and when the report of what happened goes in, we'll write it . . . unless you step aside."

With one step I was out on the boardwalk, in sight of them all. "He's not alone," I said. "I'm here, and I stand ready."

"Leave it to me, Conn," Blake said in a quiet voice.

"There's a couple there that I want," I said clearly.

But nobody was listening to me, or even looking at me. They were looking over John Blake's head and up the street to the east, and I heard horses walking . . .

a lot of them. When I looked over my shoulder, it was Red Mike I saw—Red Mike and a dozen others, all with rifles. They were the men he had brought up from Texas.

Then something moved between the buildings across the street, and I saw Meharry standing there with a shotgun in his hands. On the roof near him was Battery Mason with a rifle.

The others showed up then, and we had them surrounded. "John," Red Mike said conversationally, "you just step out of the street. We'll take it from here."

From down the street behind them Gallardo spoke. "Keep your fire in the center of the street, boys. I'll pick off any who try to get away—me and Frenchy here."

Standing there on the boardwalk, I could see the faces of McDonald and his men plain, and there were some almighty sick men out there. They were boxed —nothing left but to nail the top down.

Darrough was there, and he was standing pat, as I knew he would. He was the kind you'd have to salt down with a peck of lead before he'd stay down. I almost liked the man, but he was the man I was going to shoot first, because he was the best fighter of the lot . . . and there were some other good ones in that bunch.

"You call it, Aaron," Darrough said coolly, "and let me have Dury, over there."

"There'll be no shooting here." John Blake's voice was not loud, but it was clear as a bell, and every man-jack of us heard it. "Aaron McDonald, you're under arrest!"

The banker laughed. "Under arrest? On what charge?" He was smiling that thin little smile with his tight mouth.

"Attempted murder," John Blake said, in that same tone. "You tried to kill Kate Lundy."

For the first time it dawned on me that Aaron McDonald was wearing that black and white cowhide vest.

His face turned livid, then slowly paled, but I was scarcely noticing. For, knowing western men the way I did, I was looking at the others. And I was looking at Darrough in particular.

"Have you got proof of that, Marshal?" Darrough asked.

"Mrs. Lundy is in the doctor's office. She told me in front of the doctor that she was shot by a man wearing that vest. Conn Dury heard her say it. That vest belongs to Aaron's daughter—but he's wearing it."

Darrough dropped his rifle and reached for his belt buckle. "I'm out of it, John," he said. "I'll have nothing to do with a man who'd shoot a woman."

Guns thudded onto the ground.

"Do you want us?" Darrough said to Blake.

"No," Blake answered. "Just go to your homes and stay there."

"Hold it, Marshal," I said. "Keep Tallcott here. I want his house searched. Kate Lundy's gold was stolen in that raid."

Darrough swore. "Whoever stole that gold," he said, "needs a rope right alongside of McDonald's, and I'll tie the noose!"

Aaron McDonald had been standing his horse right there, without moving. Suddenly, almost beside me, there was a slight movement, and turning my eyes, I saw it was Linda, and she was looking at her father.

My eyes followed hers, and I saw what she saw.

No man on earth was ever more alone than Aaron McDonald at that moment. Almost without noticeable movements everyone had drawn back from him. Only

Tallcott remained near, and he was isolated, too. But neither one was thinking of the other at that moment.

Tallcott wanted to run. He looked like a whipped cur.

Aaron McDonald just sat there, because he had no place to run to. Had he been any man but the man he was, I'd have been sorry for him, for he had to stand alone before you realized how really small he was.

Money and arrogance had bought him, for a time, a certain measure of power and authority. He still had the money, but there wasn't any store, anywhere, that would take it in exchange for what McDonald needed now, nor was there any store that could supply it.

When I looked at Linda again, she was staring at her father with a positive hatred in her eyes, hatred and contempt.

"You are worse than he is," I said. "You got that boy killed, and you knew what you were doing."

She didn't even hear me. She just turned away and started back up the street. She didn't look around—not once.

CHAPTER 12

The street was deserted when day came again. Not even a lone cur dog trotted down the dusty alley between the false-fronted buildings.

The bank was closed. McDonald's Emporium was closed. Hardeman's office had been abandoned days ago, as had Bannion's saloon.

Behind three of the buildings people were loading wagons. They were silent, and if they saw me they were paying me no attention.

Rowdy Lynch had rolled in after midnight, his face black with powder smoke, grinning and happy despite a couple of minor bullet wounds . . . mere scratches.

He had been attacked about twelve miles out by a war party of young Kiowa bucks, and he'd had the time of his life. There had been about twenty in the lot, but Rowdy, though he was alone, had more than sixty loaded weapons, most of them repeating rifles.

He had water and he had plenty to eat, and when he saw them coming he ran into a big buffalo wallow and waited for them to come to him. By the time they got there he had the wagon positioned and the horses unhitched. The Kiowas were anxious not to kill the horses, for they hoped to have them for their own.

Rowdy was a good shot, and he had no worries

about ammunition, for even if he emptied his guns he
still had over a thousand rounds in the wagon . . . and
he was a man who liked a good fight. But the young
bucks thought they had a man alone who would be an
easy scalp.

They started for him, and he took a Winchester '73
and emptied seventeen shots at them. Then he
dropped it and opened fire with a .56-calibre
Spencer.

With one man and one horse down, the Kiowas
drew off to consider. They had seen only one man, but
nobody in his right mind threw lead like that. After a
bit, they tried again. Three of them came at Rowdy
from one side; the others waited, then rushed in a
body from the opposite side.

Again he laid down heavy fire with a Winchester,
followed it with a Spencer, grabbed up a shotgun and
fired four charges at the three Indians who were closing in on him.

The first blast had knocked the first Indian down,
fairly lifting him off his feet. He was dead—half
blown apart—before he hit the ground.

In all, the fight lasted five hours, with long intervals
in between. Rowdy knew the Kiowa language, and
he could distinguish some of their talk. Some were for
pulling out. They had no clear idea what sort of
trouble they had stumbled into, but they'd had
enough.

Rowdy shouted insults at them in Kiowa and talked
about ghost guns, which one of the Indians had men-
tioned. He told them the spirits of the great warriors,
enemies of the Kiowa, were all about him.

One of the Indians boasted to the others that he
would attack alone, and Rowdy sat back and let him
come. When the young warrior was almost upon him,
he opened up with a Colt revolving shotgun. There

wasn't enough left of that young Indian to carry home, and, thoroughly worried, the Kiowas pulled off and let him alone.

Standing in the street, looking up and down, I could see that the town was finished. It was Aaron Mc-Donald who had killed it, not what we had done. And Aaron McDonald was in jail, locked up and waiting to be shipped east for trial.

He had sent for his daughter, but she had not appeared. When next seen in public, she was standing waiting for the stage, two carpetbags beside her on the walk.

A man came riding up the street on a roan cow-horse, and when abreast of me he drew up. "Anybody lost a bay gelding with three white stockings . . . blaze face?"

That sounded like Red, Kate's favorite horse.

"Why?" I asked.

"Seen one like that at the crick, back yonder." He pointed toward the creek that ran by the edge of town.

"Thanks," I said.

I strolled along the street to the corral and stable, and I glanced into the stall. Sure enough, the bay gelding was gone. Saddling up, I stepped into the leather and rode down the street.

John Blake came to the door and called out to me, but I only lifted a hand. "Back in a minute!" I said, and went on.

It was a cool, pleasant morning. If those people could get their wagons rolling they could manage some miles before the heat set in.

The bay gelding was cropping grass on a green patch in the bottom, and I rode up to him and got down to pick up the halter rope. The gelding shied off a little, and I walked after the rope.

As I straightened up with it, I saw a faint hint of dust in the air along the draw to the south.

Suddenly I felt the hair prickle on the back of my neck. I stood very still, thinking quickly, as I should have been thinking before this.

How had the gelding escaped? Why—

"Hello, Dury. This here's a long way from Burro Mesa."

He had come up from behind the nearest willows, a gun in his hand. He was a tall, raw-boned man that I recalled seeing in town.

"I'm Frank Shalett. Or Hastings, if you like that better. Heard you'd killed Rich and Flange some time back, and I got kind of tired watching out for you. You've worried me some, so I think I'll see how you look when you sweat a little."

He had his gun dead center on me, and he was at pointblank range, not over forty feet away. He had been put up to me as a dead shot, and the chances of him missing at that range were slight. Yet I'd seen some good shots miss, especially when the shooter was being shot at—which he didn't expect to be.

"Nobody will ask any questions when they find you with a gun on," he said. "After all, everybody knows you're supposed to be a fast man."

This was the last of the men who had killed Jim Sotherton. How long ago that seemed! Why, I hadn't thought of hunting for him in years. Not since before the war, for I more than half believed him dead. And now he had caught up with me.

But that dust I'd seen . . . this man hadn't made that dust.

"Couldn't have been you," I said aloud. "You must have been waiting here quite a spell."

"What are you talkin' about?"

"Dust I saw in the air," I said. "Somebody else is here."

He looked disgusted. "Why, you damn' fool! You don't think I'd go for anything like that, do—"

It is harder for a man to shoot quickly to his right, so I stepped quickly left as my hand went for my gun. He shot . . . missed . . . shot again. The bullet struck me; I felt the solid blow of it and was firing myself.

Bracing myself against another bullet, I steadied my hand and put a bullet into his belly, then another. There was a spot of blood on his neck near the collar-bone, and he turned around and fell, tried to rise, and slumped back.

A voice spoke. "Now, that's what I call a fancy bit of gun play."

Where had I heard that voice before? A rifle bellowed, and the six-shooter was knocked from my hand. "And there's another bit for you. I been aimin' to even things up, even though it taken me time."

It was the Dutchman. It was that dry-gulching, sure-thing killer, Bill Hoback.

There was blood on the sand at my feet. I'd been hit, and I'd been hurt. The shock was keeping me from feeling it now, but how long would that last?

My gun was gone.

My rifle was on my saddle, and my horse was at least fifty feet away, and it might as well have been as many miles.

When he shot the pistol from my hand—no trick for such a man with a rifle at the distance—it left my arm numb to the elbow. The gun had gone spinning, and it was probably good for nothing now, anyway.

He had me, and he was going to kill me. Only he had to be sure I suffered, for I'd hurt his pride.

The boys had been right, of course. You don't let a man like that live. You kill him as you would a rattler, because he'll always be waiting around for you.

Somehow I'd gone down on one knee, and I was fuzzy about that. Had I dropped before he shot at me, or afterward?

He was back there in the brush, and he had been there when Frank Hastings, or Shalett or whatever his name was, and I shot it out. He had been waiting to see me dead, or to finish me off.

He had me cold.

Think . . . I had to think.

The boys could have heard the shooting, but not many of them, if any, were up and about. This was a morning when they could sleep and there were few such mornings for them.

"Don't figure on help. I can see that road, and if anybody starts this way I'll kill you and skedaddle. Be a while before they find out there was somebody else than you and Shalett—if they ever do."

If he could see the road, there was only one place he could be. The trouble was that he could cover every bit of the hollow where I stood from where he was hidden.

The patch of willows and cottonwood was fairly large, with some blackberry bushes among the undergrowth, which were covered with thorns that would catch and tear at a man's clothing.

My eye caught a glint of sunlight. His rifle barrel was pointed at me from alongside a tree trunk, and well back in the brush.

Frank Shalett's body lay there in front of me. Suddenly I saw a slight movement of the dead man's hand—some tightening of muscles, or relaxing. The hand had fallen across a rock when he went down, and if it moved ever so slightly again, it would fall off into the dry leaves below it.

My head was spinning, and my eyes had trouble coming to focus. Had the hand really moved?

Yes . . . it was moving again. *"Frank!"* I yelled. "Toss me the gun!"

And the hand slipped off into the leaves.

Instantly, the Dutchman shot into the dead man's body, and at the moment the gun muzzle was deflected I threw myself into the brush.

Hitting the ground, I lay absolutely still, not moving a muscle. He would be listening, and at the slightest sound I would be dead.

He might kill me, but now I had a fighting chance, if no more.

I realized that I was bleeding. The bullet must have gone into my side . . . somehow I'd had the idea it was my leg.

With infinite care I lifted my right hand and eased it, clear of the ground, back for my bowie knife. It was true I had no gun, but if I could get within reach of the knife . . .

The knife was bloody. Wiping the haft very carefully on my shirt front, I gripped it in my right hand. And I waited.

He was stalking me now.

He would be worried, because the longer he had to look for me the greater the risk of somebody coming out from town. John Blake must have heard the shots, and he would not stop at just being curious . . . by now he should be coming.

That cowhand who told me of Kate's gelding, he had been an ally of Shalett's, of course. Had he ridden on, or was he waiting in town for Shalett? If he was, he would be almighty puzzled by now.

With a stealth learned from the Apaches, I began to

inch forward. I wanted to get into a place the eye would pass over quickly. Not an obvious place for hiding . . . that would be spotted too soon, but a place practically in the open. A man lying still, unmoving, can be almost invisible.

The earth beneath me was damp, muddy from the nearby stream. Lying flat, with infinite care to make no noise, I rolled over in the mud. It would discolor my shirt, would help to make me difficult to see.

Easing myself along, I chose my spot. There was a stump and a fallen tree, and straight before them was grass, low-growing plants, and brush, none of it more than a few inches high.

By now my clothing was matted with leaves and mud, my hair was muddy, and bits of grass and leaves were clinging to it. My face was streaked with mud.

I lay down close to the edge of the brush, but almost in the open in the small clearing opposite the stump and the fallen tree, and closest to where I believed he would come.

He might see me, and if he did, I was a dead man. The eyes naturally tend to look across a clearing. He had no experience of me in the woods, and the obvious place was across the clearing where the fallen tree offered a hiding place.

Lying absolutely still, afraid even to breathe, I waited. And, my ear being against the ground, I heard him before he reached me.

He was good at stalking, and he had had plenty of experience at stalking men; he was much more skillful than most men, and therefore he was confident. He was the hunter, I the hunted.

It was a game among Apache boys to scatter out and lie down, then for others to try to see how many they could locate just by looking; and I knew how difficult it was to see someone who lay perfectly still.

He could have no doubt that he was going to kill me. My evasive tactics only prolonged the game. But he had been too successful for too long.

He came out of the brush not a dozen feet from me, his rifle half-lifted for a shot, his eyes ranging the brush on the far side of the clearing. And as he stepped past me I raised up and threw the knife upward into his left kidney.

It was hard thrown, for I am a strong man, with much practice at throwing a knife, and it went clean to the haft.

His body stiffened sharply, and I followed the knife in, catching hold of the hilt just as he started to turn. The knife came free with a hard wrench, and he tried to lift his rifle. We were face to face in that instant, our eyes only inches apart.

He looked at me with astonishment, and he said, "You've killed me!"

I said, "Uh-huh . . . it looks like it."

He fell then and lay there on the grass, staring up at me. "Take my rifle," he said, "take good care . . . finest shootin'—"

So I picked up his rifle and walked across the clearing. When I got to the far side I looked back at him. He was dead, all right, and it was hard to believe.

When I came out of the woods John Blake was bending over Shalett. Red Mike was there, too, and Meharry.

"This here's Frank Shalett," Red Mike said. "Is there somebody else back in there?"

"Uh-huh," I said, "the Dutchman's back there. If you figure to see him you'd better go look. He isn't coming out."

So they got me on a horse and took me back into town and put me in a bed.

There was one more thing I did before we started back to Texas—one more thing, I mean, after Kate and I were married. It was never in me to brag, but there were two people, I thought, who ought to know.

On a piece of note paper I wrote to Sir Richard, in England, at Sotherton Manor. The other letter I sent to Colonel Edwards, of the U. S. Army. The same message was in each letter, and it was simple enough, but I had an idea they would both understand:

First there were three, now there are none.

When we started for Texas I was riding on my back in an ambulance with Kate, but I had an idea that before we crossed the Nation I'd be back in the saddle again, looking at the world from between a horse's ears.

ABOUT THE AUTHOR

Louis L'Amour, born Louis Dearborn L'Amour, is of French-Irish descent. Although Mr. L'Amour claims his writing began as a "spur-of-the-moment thing," prompted by friends who relished his verbal tales of the West, he comes by his talent honestly. A frontiersman by heritage (his grandfather was scalped by the Sioux), and a universal man by experience, Louis L'Amour lives the life of his fictional heroes. Since leaving his native Jamestown, North Dakota, at the age of fifteen, he's been a longshoreman, lumberjack, elephant handler, hay shocker, flume builder, fruit picker, and an officer on tank destroyers during World War II. And he's written four hundred short stories and over fifty books (including a volume of poetry).

Mr. L'Amour has lectured widely, traveled the West thoroughly, studied archaeology, compiled biographies of over one thousand Western gunfighters, and read prodigiously (his library holds more than two thousand volumes). And he's watched thirty-one of his westerns as movies. He's circled the world on a freighter, mined in the West, sailed a dhow on the Red Sea, been shipwrecked in the West Indies, stranded in the Mojave Desert. He's won fifty-one of fifty-nine fights as a professional boxer and pinch-hit for Dorothy Kilgallen when she was on vacation from her column. Since 1816, thirty-three members of his family have been writers. And, he says, "I could sit in the middle of Sunset Boulevard and write with my typewriter on my knees; temperamental I am not."

Mr. L'Amour is re-creating an 1865 Western town, christened Shalako, where the borders of Utah, Arizona, New Mexico, and Colorado meet. Historically authentic from whistle to well, it will be a live, operating town, as well as a movie location and tourist attraction.

Mr. L'Amour now lives in Los Angeles with his wife Kathy, who helps with the enormous amount of research he does for his books. Soon, Mr. L'Amour hopes, the children (Beau and Angelique) will be helping too.

LOUIS L'AMOUR
1

BANTAM'S #1
ALL-TIME BESTSELLING AUTHOR
AMERICA'S FAVORITE WESTERN WRITER

☐	20257	HIGH LONESOME	$2.25
☐	14883	BORDEN CHANTRY	$2.25
☐	13606	BRIONNE	$1.95
☐	20222	THE FERGUSON RIFLE	$2.25
☐	20083	KILLOE	$2.25
☐	13602	CONAGHER	$1.95
☐	14829	NORTH TO THE RAILS	$2.25
☐	13879	THE MAN FROM SKIBBEREEN	$1.95
☐	14763	SILVER CANYON	$2.25
☐	14530	CATLOW	$2.25
☐	20033	GUNS OF THE TIMBERLANDS	$2.25
☐	14476	HANGING WOMAN CREEK	$2.25
☐	14534	FALLON	$2.25
☐	13779	UNDER THE SWEETWATER RIM	$1.95
☐	14743	MATAGORDA	$2.25
☐	14119	DARK CANYON	$1.95
☐	14882	THE CALIFORNIOS	$2.25
☐	20337	FLINT	$2.25

Buy them at your local bookstore or use this
handy coupon for ordering:

Bantam Books, Inc., Dept. LL1, 414 East Golf Road, Des Plaines, Ill. 60016

Please send me the books I have checked above. I am enclosing $_____
(please add $1.00 to cover postage and handling). Send check or money order
—no cash or C.O.D.'s please.

Mr/Mrs/Miss_____

Address_____

City_____ State/Zip_____

LL1—8/81

Please allow four to six weeks for delivery. This offer expires 2/82.

BANTAM'S #1
ALL-TIME BESTSELLING AUTHOR
AMERICA'S FAVORITE WESTERN WRITER

☐ 14931	THE STRONG SHALL LIVE	$2.25
☐ 14977	BENDIGO SHAFTER	$2.50
☐ 13881	THE KEY-LOCK MAN	$1.95
☐ 13719	RADIGAN	$1.95
☐ 13609	WAR PARTY	$1.95
☐ 20518	KIOWA TRAIL	$2.25
☐ 20460	THE BURNING HILLS	$2.25
☐ 14762	SHALAKO	$2.25
☐ 14881	KILRONE	$2.25
☐ 20139	THE RIDER OF LOST CREEK	$2.25
☐ 20265	CALLAGHEN	$2.25
☐ 20180	THE QUICK AND THE DEAD	$2.25
☐ 14536	OVER ON THE DRY SIDE	$2.25
☐ 20473	DOWN THE LONG HILLS	$2.25
☐ 20219	WESTWARD THE TIDE	$2.25
☐ 14227	KID RODELO	$1.95
☐ 20468	BROKEN GUN	$2.25
☐ 20006	WHERE THE LONG GRASS BLOWS	$2.25
☐ 14411	HOW THE WEST WAS WON	$1.95
☐ 20261	THE MAN FROM BROKEN HILLS	$2.25

Buy them at your local bookstore or use this handy coupon for ordering:

Bantam Books, Inc., Dept. LL2, 414 East Golf Road, Des Plaines, Ill. 60016

Please send me the books I have checked above. I am enclosing $_____
(please add $1.00 to cover postage and handling). Send check or money order
—no cash or C.O.D.'s please.

Mr/Mrs/Miss_____

Address_____

City_____State/Zip_____

LL2—8/81

Please allow four to six weeks for delivery. This offer expires 3/82.

SAVE $2.00 ON YOUR NEXT BOOK ORDER!

BANTAM BOOKS 🐓

Shop-at-Home
Catalog

Now you can have a complete, up-to-date catalog of Bantam's inventory of over 1,600 titles—including hard-to-find books.

And, you can save $2.00 on your next order by taking advantage of the money–saving coupon you'll find in this illustrated catalog. Choose from fiction and non-fiction titles, including mysteries, historical novels, westerns, cookbooks, romances, biographies, family living, health, and more. You'll find a description of most titles. Arranged by categories, the catalog makes it easy to find your favorite books and authors and to discover new ones.

So don't delay—send for this shop-at-home catalog and save money on your next book order.

Just send us your name and address and 50¢ to defray postage and handling costs.

BANTAM BOOKS, INC.
Dept. FC, 414 East Golf Road, Des Plaines, Ill. 60016

Mr./Mrs./Miss_____
                              (please print)
Address_____

City_____State_____Zip_____

Do you know someone who enjoys books? Just give us their names and addresses and we'll send them a catalog too at no extra cost!

Mr./Mrs./Miss_____

Address_____

City_____State_____Zip_____

Mr./Mrs./Miss_____

Address_____

City_____State_____Zip_____

FC—8/81